"Less time than that, Cap'n," said Barse. "Those vac-brains running this station don't have any idea what they're facing. And they wouldn't listen to us. That makes them worse than vac-brains. That makes them stupid—and soon to be dead."

"Trahnee might look at the data we sent." The mere mention of the woman's name sent a thrill up and down Norlin's spine. Before he could linger on the woman's memory, a shuddering vibration passed through the station, throwing him to his knees. He skidded along for several meters and crashed hard into a bulkhead. Grabbing his injured hand, he held it close. The auto-med unit had repaired him well, but deeper healing had yet to occur and leave him completely whole.

"You all right, Cap'n?"

"My hand. It feels as if I stuck it into a plasma torch."

"I'm getting strange reports from the ship," Barse said. "We've got to—"

Another tremor seized the space station and shook it until both Norlin and Barse collapsed to the deck.

"What's going on?" he demanded.

"The *Preceptor*," gasped out Barse. "Liottey got free from the surgery. The CoolinGas must have burned out parts of his brain. He fired the lasartillery and destroyed the station's docking mechanism. The ship's broken free and is drifting away."

ALSO BY ROBERT E. VARDEMAN

The Star Frontiers Trilogy

Alien Death Fleet
The Black Nebula (2011)

After the Spell Wars

Ogre Castle
The Wizard's Spell Mirror (2010)

STAR FRONTIERS 2

THE GENETIC MENACE

ROBERT E. VARDEMAN

ZUMAYA OTHERWORLDS AUSTIN TX

2010

This book is a work of fiction. Names, characters, places and incidents are products of the author's imagination or are used fictitiously. Any resemblance to actual persons or events is purely coincidental.

THE GENETIC MENACE

ISBN 978-1-934841-36-5

Look for us online at
http://www.zumayapublications.com/otherworlds

Library of Congress Cataloging-in-Publication Data

Vardeman, Robert E.
The genetic menace / by Robert E. Vardeman.
p. cm. -- (Star frontiers ; 2)
ISBN 978-1-934841-36-5 (trade paper : alk. paper) -- ISBN 978-1-934841-37-2 (electronic)
1. Space ships--Fiction. 2. Space warfare--Fiction. I. Title.
PS3572.A714G46 2010
813'.54--dc22

2010001905

For Patty, always

Chapter One

Sub-Commander Pier Norlin sat in the automated command chair of the *Preceptor* and tried to believe everything that had happened. He now captained a Nova Class cruiser, the fastest, deadliest vessel the Empire Service had in space. This command had been his reward for saving the world of Sutton II from marauding aliens' Death Fleet.

He shuddered at the memory of the vicious, bloody battle on-planet.

Norlin turned in his command chair and tipped his head to one side, playing the field of toggles and touch switches on the chair's arm like a musical instrument. The heads-up display flashed once. He blinked several times and brought up the life-size holo image of the spider-like furry-legged alien they had killed on Sutton. The spindly arms and puny hands, the hard carapace stronger than battle armor, the high-domed forehead and large dark compound eyes made it difficult to believe it was a dangerous enemy and not an oversize bug.

This insignificant fragile creature, with its comrades, had devastated planet after human-colonized planet. Their Death

Fleet scouts infiltrated a system and sabotaged celestial-approach warning sensors, then swooped down and destroyed all planetary life with their devastating radiation cannon and other energy weapons. When life had been exterminated, they landed automated looting devices that stripped the annihilated world of anything of value.

"You're looking at it again. That's not good," came a gravelly voice.

Norlin turned as a large black cat jumped into his lap. He gripped the back of the corpulent feline's neck to keep its questing paws from touching the sensitive controls. Even though most of the controls were keyed to human fingers, the cat might accidentally find the proper sequence that would damage the *Preceptor* seriously.

"Keep Neutron down in the engine room, will you, Lt. Barse?" Norlin made a face. The cat curled up in his lap and released a cloud of methane flatulence fierce enough to require everyone in the control room to turn away. "And stop feeding him so much protein."

"He eats what he likes."

"That's why he's so fat." Norlin hefted the bulky cat and handed it back to his engineer.

"I meant it about not dwelling on that." The short, stocky woman pointed at the vidscreen where Norlin still displayed the image of the spidery alien. "We've shown that we can beat them. Don't get yourself twisted around worrying about battles we haven't fought. You'll start wondering if we can do it again—and then we'll be blown into dust."

"*Vaporized* is closer to it," Mitri Sarov, the tactical officer, said. "Their radiation cannon work far better than anything we have. Our missiles have proven surprisingly ineffective against their heavier ships. They know how to armor and protect, the clever bug bastards."

Norlin smiled crookedly. The alien Death Fleet had given up one of their cannon—without knowing it. He and Tia Barse had salvaged the deadly weapon and installed it on the *Preceptor*. Although it caused grave problems when fired, draining their energy reserves to dangerous levels, it had proven itself more than a match for the aliens' top war vessels.

"Know your enemy," he said. "That's what we have to face. Admiral Bendo told us to go after them."

"The man's got vacuum for brains," muttered Chikako Miza, the ship's communications officer. "All he has to do is sit in his buried command center and fling orders around. We are the ones who have to die trying to obey them."

Barse snapped, "If you don't like it, why didn't you stay on Sutton? The admiral said he needed a com officer."

Miza shrugged, her face an emotionless mask. The sensors woven through her dark, stiff scalplock winked on and off as data relayed throughout the *Preceptor*'s bulk. Norlin wondered how the woman coordinated all the information flowing through her head and across her com board. He had seen her do the work of six at the height of combat. He wished he had a dozen like her, in spite of her cynical attitude.

"We are ordered," came Sarov's gruff, booming voice. "We obey. We are in the Empire Service. To die for our glorious Emperor Arian is all we know." The trenchant sarcasm in his voice made Miza's seem mild in comparison.

"Enough of this," Norlin barked. "We are all officers. Liking the emperor isn't required for us to do our duty."

"Just as well," grumbled Miza as her sensor lights flared all the colors of the rainbow. "He's a fool. He's worse than

Bendo. Arian never strays from Earth and his Crystal Throne."

"If that were all, I could take it better," said Barse, warming to the criticism of the emperor. Norlin knew she came from a world with strong rebel tendencies. He hoped she kept them in check. He was not going to allow a mutiny on his first real command.

"The genhanced simps he sends out are too much for me to stomach. Look what happened when one commanded the *Preceptor*. He damned near killed us all!"

To this Norlin had no reply. Barse knew he couldn't disagree, either. The genetically enhanced court surrounding the emperor showed flashes of genius, but it was always an unstable genius. Captain Pensky had commanded the *Preceptor* for a short time and had almost destroyed an entire star system—and them.

"We have our orders. If we're not doing it for the Empire Service, let's pretend we're doing it out of some sense of compassion for billions of other humans," he said, tired of their bickering. He closed his eyes and shut off the heads-up display for a moment when his first officer came into the control room.

The others in the *Preceptor*'s crew were competent—and all knew it. Gowan Liottey might carry the rank of second in command, but his abilities were clearly the least of those present. His pale-blue eyes looked watery and weak to Norlin. As cruiser commander, he tried to be fair, but Lt. Liottey was not his choice as first officer. Barse or Sarov were better choices from the criteria of ability and knowledge. For all her bitterness, Miza outclassed Liottey, too.

If pressed, Norlin knew he would have chosen the ship's cat before the sandy-haired, effeminate Liottey.

"How are we breathing?" he asked, Liottey in an attempt to make polite conversation. His readouts showed the current status of the ship's environmental systems.

"Life support systems are fully functional," the lieutenant reported.

"That's a relief," Barse said, *sotto voce*. "I'd hate to breathe vacuum and not know it."

"Engineer Barse, you have work to do. I see the shift engines are at less than one hundred percent efficiency. Mister Sarov, see to the weapons systems. When we shift back into normal space, we are going hunting for aliens. Commander Miza, monitor all com frequencies for alien chatter."

Norlin gave them busy-work to free up a few minutes with his first officer. "Mister Liottey, step over here."

The officer moved to a spot in front of the command chair. Norlin flipped a toggle and shut off this area from prying ears. He knew Chikako Miza could listen in if she desired; he had yet to stop her from eavesdropping with her clever gadgets. The impression of privacy was more important than anything else for what he had to say.

"I'm new to command," Norlin started, forming his thoughts carefully. "We've been through a great deal since I came aboard the *Preceptor*. We'll see much more combat before this ship is decommissioned."

"Sir, I'm doing my best."

"I realize that, Mister Liottey. What I want is more from you. I want more than your best. If we don't work as a completely functioning team on this ship, we'll never be arguing over whether we'll end up plasma or dust—we'll be dead."

"Sir…"

"Hear me out. More than our lives depends on how well we fight the aliens. Entire colonies must be defended."

"We can't do it alone."

"And we won't. We're doing it together." Norlin knew he wouldn't get zero-defects work from his first officer. He wouldn't even get flashes of brilliance, as he did from the others. The best Norlin could hope was for the first officer not to be responsible for their demise.

"Sir, are we going to engage soon?" asked Liottey.

"We're almost ready to shift back into normal space," Norlin said, checking his readouts. "There is every reason to believe the Renfro II system is next for invasion."

He found it impossible to keep the hardness from his voice. So many planets had been laid to waste—and so many lives lost. He forced himself to think of Neela Cosarrian—as she had been before the aliens invaded, not the emaciated husk she had become because of their attack. It had been for the best leaving her body in the cleansing fire of his rocket exhaust as he left.

"I need time to work on the escape system," Liottey said. "We can't get away from the *Preceptor* if we're hit."

"What's wrong with the escape system?"

Liottey looked confused, out of his depth. "I'm trying to find out why the firing mechanisms don't function on the escape tubes."

Norlin tipped his head to the left and got a complete readout on the escape tubes. "Why didn't you tell me this before?"

"I've been working on it, sir."

Norlin had few options open to him but to continue, knowing they had no way of getting free of the cruiser if hit. He tried to tell himself it didn't matter. The aliens were efficient and hunted down the smallest fragments from an enemy ship to insure that nothing lived.

"I can't monitor every system on this ship, Gowan," Norlin said, trying to keep the anger from showing. "That's why there are engineers, com officers, tactical weapons officers...and life maintenance officers. If you needed help, you should have asked for it. We have to work together. We're a crew—a team."

"I thought I could handle it myself," Liottey said sullenly.

"Barse will do what she can to help, if you ask her. See to it immediately. We shift out in one hour," he said. "I want the system working by then."

"What's the difference?" came Chikako Miza's voice in his helmet. "The aliens blow up even the smallest debris. Their radiation cannon are deadly against unprotected vessels. We'd never make a planet landing in those anodized coffins."

"Commander Miza, you have work to do—other than spying on me." Norlin savagely hit the toggle opening the area to full observation. To Liottey he said, "Dismissed."

Before the first officer had vanished from the control room, Norlin's headphone crackled with static, and Tia Barse said, "I don't have time to play nursemaid. I'm going to let Neutron help him. The cat's a better engineer than Gowan will ever be."

He slumped in the command chair. Aboard this ship there were no secrets—except from him, it seemed. He had so much to learn about the dynamics of society and command on a ship.

Heaving a deep sigh, he turned back to the controls. Sarov put up several different attack simulations on the vidscreen. He worked through them carefully, noting problems and strengths, trying to evaluate alien psychology. By the time Barse signaled that the engines had started cycling the *Preceptor* back into normal space, Norlin had done what he could to program his combat computer with a half-dozen different tactical plans.

"Contact," came Chikako Miza's sharp voice. "The Death Fleet is here. They've already formed an attack pattern!"

"Contact," reported Mitri Sarov, an instant later. "Locking on. Plan three in effect." The tactical officer laid down an array of missiles across a volume of space, some set to explode immediately and others that would lie doggo until they locked onto a target.

Norlin's heads-up display flared with numbers and images. He kept scaling down until he was able to take in the battle unfolding around them without drowning in details. What he saw filled him with dread. The Death Fleet had followed its standard attack strategy. Scouts crept into the Renfro II system and replaced the sensors on the perimeter designed to detect potentially dangerous incoming space debris. An undetected comet or planetesimal colliding with a civilized world would kill billions.

The aliens replaced the sensors with their own. No alien ship appeared on the controllers' screens until it was too late to mobilize an effective defense.

In too many cases, Norlin had seen this cautious approach wasn't even needed. Human defenses took too long to initiate. Too many layers of bureaucracy had to be filtered through to get permission to open fire. The aliens had wiped out humanity on each planet they attacked—until they reached Sutton II. They had been stopped there.

Norlin vowed to stop them here, too.

He checked the *Preceptor*'s sensors and tried to interpret what he saw. Sarov continued to follow the plan he had programmed, but Norlin failed to see the immediate danger. Only when the heavy cruiser's warning lights flashed and almost blinded him did he know his weapons' officers instincts had been better than his—or the *Preceptor*'s sensors.

"Coming at us from behind our flare," Sarov said. "I don't know how they positioned so quickly."

"They monitored our shift," said Miza. "I got passive checks fifteen seconds ago. They know we're here, and they'll have active probes on the way soon."

Norlin cursed. Fifteen seconds reaction time? Was that all it took the enemy to detect, position and lock onto them? The *Preceptor*'s systems took longer than that to adapt from the precipitous change from shift space to normal four-dimensional space.

"Damage negligible to all systems," came Sarov's report. "Inertial platforms turning to meet second wave attack."

Norlin felt helpless. He had approved the computer battle plans. All he could do now was sit and wait and watch.

The speed of light was almost too slow to keep up with the frantic pace of lasartillery firing, of missiles launching, of automatic preparation to use the captured radiation cannon. He shook himself and narrowed the input data stream to his display again, focusing on Chikako Miza's communications reports.

The alien vessel was small, yet it gave them more than their share of trouble. Half a dozen internal systems had failed during the first assault. Norlin ignored the failures and concentrated on the parts that had made it through unscathed. The *Preceptor* still functioned and fought well enough to survive.

"They're not budging," came Miza's calm, almost mechanical voice. The sensors woven into her tall, stiff scalplock flickered on and off faster than Norlin could focus on them. Whatever information they gave allowed her to keep up with the ever-changing conditions both inside the *Preceptor* and outside among the alien Death Fleet.

"The bugs came up right on our tail. They're locked onto us and firing."

Norlin switched to the weapons display and saw that the solitary attacking alien scout vessel had changed tactics. As long as their rocket flare pointed toward the enemy ship, missiles locked on easily and were difficult to destroy in flight.

"We're swinging around," he announced. "Let's get some hardware into play." A half-dozen of the *Preceptor*'s missiles blew apart a new wave of torpedoes from the alien scout. "Tia, how's the radiation cannon?"

"Do we have to use it?" she asked. "It puts us down for too long. We'd need at least a day to recharge. Maybe more, if we're not lucky."

Norlin checked the battle's progress and decided not to use the captured cannon. Miza had detected another alien scout ship less than twenty light-minutes away. It could reach them at sub-light speed before they could recharge and prepare for another assault.

The ship seemed to slide, as if it were a wheeled giant and had slipped in mud. Norlin touched a private com link and spoke directly to his first officer.

"Forget the escape tubes. Get an RRU to work on the hull. We're leaking like a damned sieve."

"I've already got a robot repair unit at work, sir," came Liottey's whining voice. "It's not working fast enough to keep up with the damage we're taking."

"Put another one to work, then. Keep us airtight." Norlin savagely toggled off. He needed a new second-in-command. Gowan Liottey left everything to chance.

While Sarov worked on the immediate problem of defeating the alien scout, Norlin turned his attention to the second ship. Communication between elements of the Death Fleet was minimal before an attack to prevent humans from overhearing. During an attack, they coordinated perfectly. He tried to determine if this scout was in contact with any other.

Pier Norlin tapped in a new tactical plan to deal with the distant scout ship, if it bothered to come to its companion's aid. The *Preceptor* shuddered as an array of missiles launched. He blanketed the intervening space with a statistically perfect web of slowly patrolling low-power high-explosive missiles. If the alien joined the attack, it would find itself under attack from all quarters.

Satisfied, he turned his attention back to the current battle. He swore under his breath when he saw how the *Preceptor*'s condition had worsened. A missile had penetrated their defensive array and ruptured the hull near the radiation cannon nodule. The weapon was still functional, but reaching it without a spacesuit would be impossible.

"Liottey, get another RRU to work. Put a dozen to work, if that's what it takes."

"Let me do it, Cap'n," came Barse's voice in his ear. "Gowan is making matters worse with his dumb programming. I tell you, the cat can do a better job."

"Let Neutron do it, then. Get those air leaks fixed." Norlin watched nervously as Barse sent her engine room RRUs forward into the damaged area. The control room had its own shielding and air supply and could survive even if most of the cruiser were destroyed. What worried Norlin was losing the capability offered by the radiation cannon.

"Plan three is failing, two sigma probability of defeat within the hour."

"Recommendation?" he snapped at his tactical officer. Sarov punched in a new program. Norlin approved it after a cursory examination. He had faith in the man's abilities.

"One strike on enemy," came Miza's voice. Norlin checked his heads-up display and saw damage estimates. The alien scout ship wasn't totally out of commission, but a second direct hit would destroy it. He watched the vidscreen as three of the *Preceptor*'s missiles struck simultaneously.

"Enemy defeated," came Sarov's stolid, emotionless voice. "Checking weapons systems in anticipation of second scout ship attacking."

Norlin ran the battle recording through his tactical computer and made alterations to the expert system program that had guided them originally. Only through continual updating could they hope to defeat the Death Fleet. The aliens had superior firepower, battle coordination and—usually—the element of surprise. That didn't leave much but innovation as Norlin's primary weapon.

The *Preceptor* had left the battle in good shape. The other alien ship would prove no more difficult an obstacle.

"Chikako, contact the Renfro Port Authority and warn them of the Death Fleet's presence. Tell them their perimeter sensors are not to be trusted. Have them go to laser radar and optical observation. The usual warning."

"Yes, sir, lidar and opticals. Message sent."

Norlin sank back in his command chair. He adjusted his display to pick up the Renfro II response. His stomach turned over when he saw it. He was already punching in a direct comlink by the time Chikako Miza relayed the answer.

"They don't believe there is any danger, sir."

"Just like the other systems," he said grimly. "How can we make them believe us?"

“Scout ship on intercept course,” broke in Sarov. “Estimated time for battle—one hour.”

It never changed. Pier Norlin did what he could to convince the Port Authority of their plight. That usually proved to be the more difficult battle to fight.

The Empire Service’s heaviest cruiser barely defeated the smallest scout ship in the Death Fleet—again. Only then did Norlin set course for the space station circling Renfro II and the never-ending battle with bureaucracy.

Chapter Two

"We'll all die!"

Pier Norlin touched the OFF switch on his heads-up display and glared at Gowan Liottey. The first officer had failed to perform his duties adequately during the battle. Now that the threat had passed and the two alien scout ships were debris floating between the planets, his behavior was even less acceptable.

"Lieutenant!" snapped Norlin. "I'll order your tongue cut out if you don't shut up."

"You can't. Sir, we're losing atmosphere. We'll be dead in an hour." Liottey tore at his hair and dropped to the deck, sobbing hysterically.

Of Barse, Norlin asked, "What's wrong with him?"

"We took a hit in the coolant system. He's sniffed too much CoolinGas."

"Why wasn't he wearing a spacesuit or a respirator? That stuff is dangerous."

The chief engineer looked him squarely in the eye and shook her head.

Norlin sighed. "Get him to sick bay and let the auto-med go over him. Pump his lungs, scrub his blood, do whatever has to be done to get him back into shape. Don't let him in the control room again until he's ready."

"Does this mean Liottey's out of the chain of command?" asked Sarov.

"You're next in command," Norlin said. "Just don't think about assassinating the captain to get ahead." He spoke with a hint of warning. Throughout the Empire Service, rumors were rife that assassination was a common practice closer to Earth and the emperor's court.

"I will try to remember that you cautioned me," Mitri Sarov said impassively. Norlin couldn't tell if the man's neutral tone was meant as a joke or should be taken seriously.

He waited until Liottey had been escorted from the control room, then turned on his displays once more. A quick review of the major systems showed nothing seriously wrong. The hull leaks that had sent his first officer into a panic were minor and were being taken care of by a half-dozen RRUs programmed by Tia Barse.

"Coolant system is acting up," he said, using his throat mike. "I don't want the CoolinGas getting into the filtration system. We don't have time to counter its effects—better to keep it out in the first place." He turned his attention elsewhere, saw that the other officers had finished their repairs and checks and then lost himself in a replay of the battle.

The second scout ship had been easily vanquished. The missile array he had laid out worked well against the overconfident alien. Three of the low-power missiles had escaped detection. As the alien ship rocketed past, they had activated and come in from behind, hidden from easy detection by the alien's own rocket flare. The maneuver worked as well for a human war vessel as it did an alien. Before battle even had been joined, the alien scout ship had sustained too much damage to be a menace.

Sarov had taken care of the vessel with a single blast from their forward lasartillery battery.

"We won't need much dry-dock time, since repairs will be minimal this time," Norlin said. "Be sure to watch carefully whoever Renfro Port Authority sends aboard. No one even looks at the radiation cannon without my permission."

"We are not fools, Captain," Miza said sarcastically. "Not like poor Gowan."

Norlin sighed. He had risen in rank too quickly to be able to handle such outright disobedience. He had checked the Empire Service records and found he was the youngest officer commanding a line vessel—such were the pressures of a genocidal war that most of the worlds didn't even know was being waged. The officers who hadn't been killed on those worlds where they *did* know had deserted. Norlin was one of only a handful of remaining pilots on the far frontier. A few years experience commanding smaller vessels would have stood him in good stead. but he had to squeeze a dozen years of seasoning into a few weeks.

That the *Preceptor* confronted and destroyed ships in the alien fleet showed he was not entirely out of his depth. The bickering and political maneuvering among the crew lay beyond his control to stop, however. He had learned in the Empire Service Academy that internal problems destroyed more ships than any threat from an enemy, but for too many years the fleet had seen little more than garrison duty, with no real adversaries. The rot that began on some worlds desiring autonomy from the Empire had never been addressed because the Emperor refused to look beyond his court on Earth. Norlin had to grapple with both a fearsome enemy and colonial disobedience and could not expect much support from the Empire Service.

"Captain, the Port Authority is refusing us a docking port unless we have authorization from...I can't make it out."

Norlin shook himself out of his reverie and tried to understand what his communications officer had said. An Empire Service space station refusing a cruiser immediate docking was unheard-of.

"Send a Class One priority signal."

"I did. They refuse to acknowledge." Miza's sensors flashed all the colors of the rainbow and finally settled on a dull blue that was more menacing than pure red. Norlin wondered what she was trying to do that required so much of her circuitry. He started to ask, then decided against it. Much of what the *Preceptor*'s officers did to perform their duties bordered on the illegal. Tia Barse once had seduced an engineer to get parts needed for repair. Norlin didn't want to think what Sarov might do if someone thwarted him. The stolid tactical officer was built like a main battle tank and had a mind like a superspeed computer.

He listened to the byplay between Miza and the Renfro II Port Authority. Gradually, he understood the problem, accessed the ship's computer and got the sketchy information about the Renfro system.

He had assumed wrongly that the planet was densely populated. The single flag it carried in the data bank showed an ammonia-and-methane atmosphere unfit for direct human colonization. The rare earth mines on the planet made Renfro II worthy of all the attention that could be lavished on it. Yttrium, necessary for constructing superconducting ceramics, was plentiful a half-kilometer under the planet's rocky crust.

"We understand that the planet is off-limits," he cut in. "We are requesting only space station docking and the opportunity to speak with the planetary governor or stationmaster."

"Why?" came the sharp question.

Norlin began to lose his temper. "This is Empire Service Cruiser *Preceptor* on a mission of highest priority. I demand to be given a berthing assignment immediately."

"Demand all you want. We've got lasartillery that can hold you off."

"Have they mutinied?" asked Sarov. "No one refuses a cruiser. We can blow them out of the sky in ten minutes—in less than a second if we use the radiation cannon. I've got a lock on their defensive system. We can slide past, and they'll never know what happened."

"Port Authority..." Norlin began.

"Wait a microsec, can you? I've got some music on and want to hear the end of the piece."

Norlin's finger almost touched the switch that would have launched a missile at the space station. He held back, fuming. The Port Authority controller was annoying him purposely. He wanted to know why.

"Are you aware of the Death Fleet's scouts at this system's perimeter? The main body of the alien invasion force might arrive at any time."

"Death Fleet? You've been watching too many of the emperor's vidramas."

Norlin left open his com-link as he spoke to his tactical officer. "Mr. Sarov, prepare a low-destruct array. Take out the controller's office. Try to leave the rest of the space station intact, as much as you can. But don't waste too much time on that."

"What of their lasartillery?"

"Counter-measures, as necessary," Norlin said. To be sure the controller understood, he asked, "Are you remaining in your office or have you left?"

"I'm still here." The cockiness had vanished. "There's no way you'd fire on this station."

"Give me docking permission, or you'll find out. I say again, this is Empire Service Cruiser *Preceptor* on a mission of grave importance to you and everyone in the Renfro II system."

"We'll send out a tug to pull you into port three." A long pause filled with static from a building solar storm, then: "Would you have fired? Really?"

"Stand down the missiles, Mr. Sarov." Norlin made sure the missiles his tactical officer had prepared were put back on safety. "All hands, prepare to dock with the station."

He watched with grim satisfaction as the small space tug came out and attached magnetic lines to steel towing plates mounted in the composite hull. Within five minutes they were berthed, and in ten he and Tia Barse were swimming down the space station's zero-g central axis toward the commander's office.

"There's no reason to get upset, Cap'n," said Barse. "You just ran afoul of a petty bureaucrat. You know now how it feels."

He glared at her, refusing to answer her oblique charge. The station's spin tugged at him and gradually he felt the centrifugal force pulling his feet to the outer wall. He found it difficult to stalk angrily in low-g, but he did his best. He didn't even slow down when the human secretary tried to ask his business.

He shoved through into the commander's office. A thin, almost emaciated man sat behind the desk, his eyes bright.

Norlin recoiled at the sight of such feverish intensity. The translucent hands fluttered constantly, like dried leaves trapped in a high wind. But the eyes held him. The deep, dark pits were touched with madness.

"You wouldn't have blown up the Port Authority controller's officer, would you?" asked the skeletal man.

"Yes, dammit, I would have. The controller in charge should be disciplined immediately. He was endangering the entire space station."

"I was in charge. I'm the controller."

"What?" Norlin glanced at Barse, who only shook her head. "The station commander acts as controller, too?" This was unheard-of, even on frontier worlds where humans were scarce. The jobs were different, and each too demanding for one man to deal with alone.

"No, but the station commander is…elsewhere."

"Get him here. I must talk to him," Norlin said.

"Who are you to come jetting in here and demanding to see him? *Who?*"

Norlin stepped back from the thin man and wondered at the rage pent-up in him. More than simple anger radiated from the controller; Norlin felt an insanity like a palpable force.

"Cap'n," muttered Barse. "Is he genhanced?"

"*Him?*"

"He looks it. Remember how Pensky got just before he did something really demented?"

"Yes," the gaunt man shouted. "I am genhanced and proud of it. I'm Emperor Arian's third cousin."

"Everyone is related at the Earth court," Norlin said with distaste.

That the scientists played with genes didn't bother him unduly. It irritated him that the failures were shipped to the frontier—and caused situations such as the one he now faced. With genhanced genius all too often went instability and outright insanity.

"I am the emperor's favorite cousin. Really, I am. He sent me to Renfro to watch over the others."

"The station commander?"

"Yes! I spy on Delamier and his slut sister. They aren't fit to run an on-planet whorehouse, much less this fine space station."

"Where are they?" asked Barse.

"You're with them. You're in league with them to kill me!"

Norlin shrugged and twisted his forearm slightly. A small laser pistol dropped into his grip from a hidden spring mechanism. The weapon had little stopping power, but a few quick bursts might cut off the controller's legs, if it came to that.

"No, no, we're not," soothed Barse. The heavy-set woman moved to the far side of the room, drawing the controller's attention. Norlin shifted slowly to get behind the genhanced man. Killing him might not be necessary if he could be subdued quickly.

"You're tricking me!" the controller shouted, jumping with unnatural agility over the desk and landing on all fours in the center of the floor. "You and Delamier and Trahnee are jealous because I'm related to Emperor Arian and you're not. I'm his favorite. He told me!"

"Jealous, no. Envious, yes," said Norlin, moving back around the desk. "Tell us about him. Tell us about the Crystal Throne. What is it like? Is it as grand as everyone says?" He worked to keep the man's attention on harmless topics. If he couldn't grab the controller, Barse would.

"Die!" the genhanced shrieked. He grabbed for something hidden inside his ill-fitting lime green tunic.

Norlin reacted swiftly. He raised his small laser and fired—and shrieked in agony as the weapon exploded in his hand.

"Damper field in the office, Cap'n," said Barse. "I don't know how they hid it. I didn't detect anything when we came in." She rested her hand on a small instrument pack at her hip.

"I need medical attention," he said, grimacing. Two of his fingers hung by strips of flesh. Blood gushed from a severed artery and turned him weak in the knees. He sank to the desk-top. Even this didn't provide enough support.

"Live by the sword, die by the sword," cackled the controller. The man jerked free from his tunic a tiny black box with a single display light winking on the side. "You're all going to die—because I command it!"

Barse started for him, then stopped when his finger punched down hard on the contact. The light flashed faster, then went out.

"What is it?" she asked, grabbing the skeletal man by the throat. She lifted him easily from the floor until only his toes brushed the metal surface. "What did you activate?"

"I'll never tell!"

"You'll be dead before anything happens," Barse warned. Norlin tried to speak. He could only clutch at his damaged hand and try not to pass out.

"He's dead *now*," came a cold voice.

A sharp crackle of electrical discharge was followed by the controller's gasp. He went limp in Barse's grip. She dropped him to the floor and faced the man and woman standing in the door.

"We've already summoned an auto-med unit for your captain." The tall woman appeared unruffled by the blood pooling on the floor. Her grey eyes were fixed on the controller. A brief expression of contempt touched her thin lips before they shifted into an insincere smile. "You did well with Kortani. He had a spark of...genius."

"He was a vacuum-brained—"

"Barse," groaned Norlin. "Never mind. What happened?"

The tall woman drifted closer, her eyes flickering across his wounds and then coming back to lock with his light-violet ones. "Kortani made the mistake of believing himself superior."

"He was genhanced," gasped out Norlin. He stiffened when the silent auto-med unit clamped his wrist firmly and began tending to the severed fingers and wildly pumping artery.

"He made that claim," the woman said. "Perhaps he was. I doubt he ever saw the Crystal Throne or had even been to Earth. He was definitely not Emperor Arian's cousin."

"How do you know?"

"Bo and *I* are the emperor's favorites."

"Bo?" Norlin strengthened as the auto-med unit clicked and whirred and worked medical miracles on his hand. Feeling returned to his fingers. He flexed them and experienced a twinge of pain that faded quickly. He tensed them and balled them into a fist. Even the severed artery had been repaired by the efficient medical robot.

"Bo Delamier, the station commander."

The man who had until now stood silently behind the woman bowed deeply. For Norlin's taste, the action carried too much arrogance. He had seen such superior airs before in members—or would-be members—of the emperor's court.

"I am charged with guarding the mines below us. Perhaps poor Kortani was too instilled with zeal to perform this noble task." Delamier's words carried more than a hint of mockery.

Norlin held up his repaired hand to cut off Barse's irate reply. He knew such effrontery sparked deep-seated anger in her. She made no secret of her rebel leanings, even as she worked as an Empire Service officer on the cruiser.

"I've ordered my communications officer to transfer full data on the impending invasion of the Renfro system. With it are photos and depositions covering the Death Fleet's action on Sutton II and other worlds."

"Death Fleet?" Delamier's words had been dipped in the acid of sarcasm. "How melodramatic, isn't it, Trahnee?"

"The aliens are advanced technologically but depend primarily on surprise in battle. We can defeat them. We did on Sutton. Full details—"

"Never mind such nonsense. What is it you want on my station?" asked Delamier. "We might comply if it isn't too outrageous, then you can go about your mission."

"My *mission*, Commander, is to protect Empire Service colonies. Renfro is next on the alien invasion schedule, though I cannot imagine why, since the atmosphere is poisonous."

"The minerals we mine on-planet are rather important," Trahnee said.

Norlin stared at her. At first he had thought she was somewhat plain. Now he wasn't sure. She had a tall, regal carriage and an air of elegance. He couldn't call it beauty—not quite. But he felt something approaching excitement when he stared into her grey eyes. They pulled him inward, downward into her very soul.

He shook this strangely intimate feeling off. "We destroyed two scouts after they replaced your perimeter sensors. We have full combat data, if you want to see it."

"Impossible," scoffed Delamier. "It's not possible to tamper with my sensors. I would know it instantly."

"They replaced your detectors with their own. The Death Fleet will arrive and position itself before you know you're under attack."

"Not likely," said Delamier. "You have been in space far too long. Perhaps we can show you a bit of recreational amusement to put the edge back on your skills."

"Commander, the alien fleet is real. Examine the data." Norlin touched the com-link on his belt. Chikako Miza transferred the full data package into the space station's computer banks. "It's available. We may not have much time."

"We have all the time in the world," said Trahnee. "That's one of the drearier aspects of being on the frontier. There is so little to do to interrupt the boredom."

"It'll get a lot more interesting soon," muttered Barse, her jaw set and her eyes cold. "Cap'n, let's get the hell out of here and let them be blown into dust."

Norlin almost agreed with his engineer when he saw the insolent sneer Delamier gave them. The space station commander thought they were nothing more than stupid colonials. Only someone from the emperor's court could possibly show such disregard for the facts.

His attention went from Delamier to Trahnee. He shook himself. She seemed so much more attractive than the first time he had seen her. Not beautiful. Not that, but...appealing.

"Do run along, you two. I can manage the station quite well without your opinions on system defenses."

"The aliens will arrive. Maybe not today or tomorrow, but soon. They never deviate from their established battle plan. Check your perimeter sensors—now."

"Yes, yes, of course." Delamier waved them away. Trahnee watched with cool, pale eyes that probed Norlin's emotional depths.

Norlin started from the room, glad to be away from the uncomfortable examination. He halted when his com-link beeped. He turned to Delamier and said, "Don't bother with the sensors."

"Oh?" Delamier lifted one eyebrow in a superior expression. "Recanting your wild tale of murderous aliens?"

"No. My weapons officer just picked up the Death Fleet's braking radiation. Fourteen hundred warships just shifted into normal space and will be here within a day. You'd better prepare for immediate evacuation and escape to another colony."

Trahnee went to a terminal and saw confirmation of Norlin's claim about the Bremsstrahlen. Every x-ray detector on the space station's hull had gone wild. She shrugged, as if saying, *What now?*

Delamier laughed as if he had heard the finest joke ever told. "Evacuation? Don't be absurd. We'll fight. This will be the most delightful diversion we've had since arriving at this miserable place. Trahnee, let us devise a devastatingly clever defensive scheme to defeat these…aliens. We fight!"

Norlin shuddered. Delamier was another of the emperor's genhanced court who had slipped over the border between sanity and madness.

Chapter Three

The blaring warning sirens caused Pier Norlin to clap his hands reflexively over his ears to shut out the racket. He almost wished for an atmosphere leak to cut the terrible din to a tolerable level.

He and Barse had gotten only halfway to the docking bay and the *Preceptor* when the alarms deafened him.

"Why are they doing this?" she shouted. Even standing only a meter away, he barely heard her.

He shook his head as if this might get rid of the loud ringing noises. The standard procedure for battle warning was a single siren and flashing lights. A sudden hull breach and an atmospheric leak could prevent some personnel from hearing an audible signal. For whatever reason, Delamier preferred this earsplitting uproar.

"Let's get to the ship. I don't want to stay here a second longer, because this station is going to be a cloud of expanding plasma in a few hours." He hoped his ears weren't permanently damaged by the cacophony.

"Less time than that, Cap'n," said Barse. "Those vac-brains running this station don't have any idea what they're facing. And they wouldn't listen to us. That makes them worse than vac-brains. That makes them stupid—and soon to be dead."

"Trahnee might look at the data we sent." The mere mention of the woman's name sent a thrill up and down Norlin's spine. Before he could linger on the woman's memory, a shuddering vibration passed through the station, throwing him to his knees. He skidded along for several meters and crashed hard into a bulkhead. Grabbing his injured hand, he held it close. The auto-med unit had repaired him well, but deeper healing had yet to occur and leave him completely whole.

"You all right, Cap'n?"

"My hand. It feels as if I stuck it into a plasma torch."

"I'm getting strange reports from the ship," Barse said. "We've got to—"

Another tremor seized the space station and shook it until both Norlin and Barse collapsed to the deck.

"What's going on?" he demanded.

"The *Preceptor*," gasped out Barse. "Liottey got free from the surgery. The CoolinGas must have burned out parts of his brain. He fired the lasartillery and destroyed the station's docking mechanism. The ship's broken free and is drifting away."

Norlin tried to reach his own com-link and failed. The fingers on his right hand refused to close on the toggle. Awkwardly, he touched it with his left. It didn't do him any good. The unit had been damaged when he fell.

"Give me yours. Now, dammit." He snatched Barse's com-link and activated it. "Sarov, report."

Static crackled and popped, but the tactical officer's voice came through clearly enough. He sounded unperturbed.

"Liottey's locked himself in the forward laser battery, Captain. The coolant gas has impaired his judgment. The auto-med unit report shows cortical damage, possibly permanent."

"That's making him act like a madman?"

"He's never been totally rational, Captain," came Sarov's dour reminder. "Permission to evacuate the chamber."

"You'll kill him if you do that!"

Sarov didn't answer. Norlin cursed. He leaned back against the smooth, cool bulkhead and wondered what to do. Losing his first officer in such a manner, under these conditions, might be enough to get him court-martialed. A captain was responsible for all aspects of his ship's condition—and the behavior of his crew.

He toggled the com-link again. "Sarov, report on ship's status."

"Airlock damage is minimal. The space station sustained more damage than we did when the lasers fired. We're fifteen thousand kilometers from the station and orbital speed is decreasing. We'll slip into a higher orbit unless we make corrections soon."

"Give me the status on the Death Fleet."

"Three light-minutes away and closing. Deceleration rates plotted. They'll achieve Renfro II orbit within twenty hours."

Before Norlin could issue the command to return and pick them up, the space station shuddered again. This time he recognized source of the tremors.

"Delamier! He opened fire on the *Preceptor*. Those are the station's lasartillery batteries."

"I'm afraid you're right, Cap'n." Barse knelt and tried to help him to his feet, but the increasing station gyrations caused her to lose her balance and rejoin him on the deck.

"Sarov, evasive action. Avoid the station's fire. Don't return fire under any circumstances. We'll get things cleared up on this end. Evacuate the chamber. Stop Liottey." Norlin closed his eyes and swallowed hard. He had just ordered his first officer's death. If only he'd had more time, if only he had not been under such pressure from Delamier and the Death Fleet, if only…

Scrambling to get his feet under him, Norlin hurried back to the station commander's office. He stepped over Kortani's lifeless body and ducked into the room. Trahnee stood at one side, a faint smile on her lips. He didn't understand her reaction. Bo Delamier sat behind the desk, the full vidscreen and control panel capabilities activated in front of him.

"Your ship blew off a portion of the station," Delamier said. "Are you the attacking Death Fleet or is this some bizarre, demented colonial behavior?"

"My first officer is suffering from brain damage," Norlin said.

"A trait shared by other officers in your command?" asked Trahnee, amused.

"Use your lidar. My tac officer reports the Death Fleet decelerating less than three light-minutes away. You can pick up the radiation from their shift braking."

"There *is* an unusual amount of hyperlight radiation," commented Trahnee, as if it were a trivial datum and not worth further consideration.

"We really might be under attack, my dear. This can be what we've waited for ever since arriving at this wearisome station."

Delamier smiled at her. Norlin tried to interpret what passed between the two but couldn't. It was more than commander to subordinate officer, yet less than an intimate body-language message.

"Abandon the station," Norlin urged. "You can't fight them. There are fourteen hundred ships in their fleet. The smallest scout ship is more than a match for your full defensive fire."

"We've made modifications," Delamier said. "It gets dreary out here tending the robot mines below."

"There are some humans down there," Trahnee cut in. "They come up for R-and-R occasionally and make life less tedious."

"But they are lower class," said Delamier. "Even with your base appetites, you must admit that."

"Delamier! The aliens are going to be here soon. Get your defenses powered up, if you refuse to run."

"We'd have to abandon almost two hundred miners on the planet," Trahnee said, as if thinking aloud. "They wouldn't like that. And there are some engaging people among them. What a loss."

"The space station," pleaded Norlin. "Abandon it or defend it. There's not much time."

"Time?" said Delamier, as if noticing him for the first time. "We have enough. We'd have even more if your wayward first officer hadn't damaged so much of my space station. I've sent RRUs to fix what they can."

"All the robot repair units in the Empire Service won't help once the Death Fleet arrives."

"They'll get a surprise. This might appear a poor, undefended system, but it isn't. Yttrium mining is quite profitable. That's why Emperor Arian sent us all the way out here to oversee it. Bo has diverted some of the profits from the venture to reinforce the station's defensive structure."

Norlin's hopes soared. Had these two dilettantes really built a defensive system equal to that of the Empire Service sector base on Sutton II? The aliens might be defeated again!

"What are your capabilities?" he asked.

"That's Bo's field, not mine," said Trahnee. She chuckled , as if in amusement at the notion of having anything to do with armaments.

"We have a half-dozen laser batteries trained and ready for action," Delamier said smugly.

"A half-dozen!" blurted Barse. "Against fourteen hundred ships?"

Delamier laughed. "You'll see how effective they are with expert guidance."

"Get us back to the *Preceptor*, Cap'n. I'd rather die on board my own ship than here."

Norlin swung around to the command terminal and leaned past Delamier. "*Preceptor*, come in. Sarov, can you return and pick us up?"

Heavy static masked the reply. Norlin fiddled with the controls and got a laser com-link to his ship.

"Sorry, Captain. We're under attack. A small scout came around the planet in a lower orbit, moving fast, and came up under us. A dozen missiles launched—Sarov is still working to intercept the last of them," reported Chikako Miza.

"What about Liottey?" he asked. Norlin worried more about the lack of crew aboard his cruiser than Sarov's ability to intercept a few missiles. "Is he dead?"

"He's still in the forward battery. I've cut off his power. We evacuated the chamber, but he has a spacesuit."

"*Now* he wears his suit," complained Barse.

"What," Norlin asked, "is his status?"

"Isolated. We can operate without him." Miza broke off for a moment, then returned. "We cannot redock with the station. Heavy enemy activity from alien advance units prevents it."

"We're marooned with these space cases?" Barse stared at Delamier and Trahnee in horror.

"Can you speed up, get into a lower orbit and then redock with the station?" asked Norlin. He didn't want to be stranded on the space station any more than his engineering officer did.

"We have no way of estimating enemy force on the far side of the planet. It might prove impossible, Captain."

"Here," said Delamier. "Look at our reports." He punched up a complete system chart showing tiny red dots on the far side of Renfro II.

"Those are enemy vessels?" asked Norlin.

"They're not identified, so we must assume so," Delamier said, relishing the situation far more than Norlin. "At least ten ships are out there. However did they get so close without us noticing them before? Do you have any notion, my dear?"

Trahnee shook her head, looking concerned for the first time.

"They replaced your sensors with their own, you damned fool!" raged Barse.

"Trahnee, have her incarcerated. Or throw her out the airlock. I refuse to be insulted by lower life forms in my own space station," said Delamier.

"Wait," said Norlin. "We're under stress."

"Why?" asked Delamier. "This is fun." He seemed sincere in his delight. Norlin tried to ignore him as he studied the control board. The panel contained a half-dozen unfamiliar segments.

"What do those do?" he asked. He reached for one to activate its status report. Delamier's strong hand grabbed his wrist and pulled him away.

"These so-called aliens of yours—the Death Fleet," he said sarcastically. "They will be in for a fine surprise from me. The emperor's trust is well placed in my ability to defend this horrible planet."

Norlin looked to Trahnee. She smiled knowingly and nodded.

"He *is* competent," she said. For some reason, Norlin believed her. "These ships have no chance for survival. You realize, of course, your ship will be destroyed, too, when the defensive shield is activated."

"Can you ignore the *Preceptor*?" he asked.

"What shield?" cut in Barse. "There can't be a force shield strong enough to hold back the aliens' weapons. Their radiation cannon is—" She quieted when she saw the dark look on Norlin's face.

"I suppose we can program in a small hole for your pitiful little ship to slip through. Yes, here it is. See?" Delamier worked on his keyboard until a single green light winked on and off.

Norlin tried to assimilate the information flowing across the control board. Delamier played the instruments expertly. More and more red lights blazed on the panel. Each alien ship monitored on the far side of the planet popped up on the vidscreen, a glowing white ring circling it.

"He has them all located and pinpointed by the defense computer," Trahnee said softly, as if speaking might disturb a master at work. "It is only a matter of minutes before he destroys them. The threat will be gone then."

"The main body of the Death Fleet is still on the way," Barse said. "Even on Sutton we didn't touch them. Admiral Bendo had—"

"Quiet," snapped Delamier. "I need to concentrate." His strong chin trembled as he chewed on his lower lip. His eyes narrowed as he studied the readouts.

Trahnee took Norlin's arm and pulled him to one side of the office. "You will find this instructive. The ships will all be destroyed in a few seconds. Tell me, Captain, whose vessels are they? Rebels? Emperor Arian told us many worlds were in rebellion. This is exciting."

"They're not rebels," Norlin said, unable to take his eyes off the control board. Only one dot remained uncircled—he hoped the green spot was the *Preceptor*. He didn't think the space station had the firepower to destroy this many aliens, but he found Trahnee's quiet confidence contagious. He dared to hope.

"Cap'n, there's a power drain on the station meters. Look."

Norlin tried to understand all that was happening. He couldn't.

"Bo, do it soon," Trahnee said, more sharply than she had spoken to him previously. "Don't dally."

"Yes, my dear, yes...yes...now!" Delamier's finger stabbed down on a pressure-sensitive plate. Each red circle on the vidscreen turned into an eye-searing point of virulent energy. Norlin threw up his arm to shield his eyes. Pain lanced up and into his right shoulder from the abrupt movement.

When he was able to see again without the spots dancing in front of his eyes, he saw only a solitary green spot on the vidscreen. Delamier smiled.

"See?" the station commander said in a superior tone. "They're gone. My defensive system worked as I knew it would. Those rebels were no threat at all."

Norlin found it hard to believe, but he had to accept what the readouts told him. Bo Delamier had destroyed a dozen alien scout ships with a single command.

Could he destroy the main elements of the Death Fleet? Norlin hoped so. Their lives depended on it.

Chapter Four

They did it," Tia Barse said, a hint of awe in her voice. "We've been up against those bastards and barely escaped. They destroyed a full dozen alien ships and didn't break a sweat."

Trahnee smiled beatifically. Norlin basked in that smile, knowing it was directed at him alone. He studied the woman more carefully, the pressure of attack gone. His first impression changed. She wasn't the most beautiful woman he had ever seen, but she had a quality about her that transcended mere physical appearance. He tried to compare her to Neela but somehow couldn't quite remember what it had been about his lover that had been so intriguing.

"You are astounded at our easy victory, Captain Norlin? You shouldn't be. Bo and I are genhanced. None stands against us when we put our full talents to use."

"I'm an electronic genius," Delamier boasted. "This defensive system shields the planet from any possible attack."

"What did you do?" Norlin asked. "How did you destroy the aliens?"

"I saw in your report how the Sutton commander used fighting mirrors on a moon." Delamier sniffed in contempt. "So primitive, even if it did appear to work for a short while. My configuration of battle elements is more efficient."

"You've read my report? But you—" Norlin cut off his protest, confused. He hadn't noticed either Trahnee or Bo Delamier reading the report put into the space station's data bank.

"Poor Pier," Trahnee said. She laid her hand on his shoulder. "You've never been around genhanced officers, have you? We read very fast."

"It took less than five seconds to go through your rather skimpy data," said Delamier. "Most of it proved redundant. I condensed the data to a knowledge kernel, then began thinking."

"A knowledge kernel?" asked Norlin.

"Our terminology, Pier. It means nothing to you—it can't," Trahnee said. Norlin bristled at the implication of this technique being beyond his feeble grasp. Somehow, the way she looked at him and smiled gently ameliorated the sting.

"We assimilate vast amounts of information quickly. That is why your aliens are now dust."

"What about the rest of them?" asked Barse. "These were helpless ships in comparison to their planet beamers. They turn their radiation weapons on a world and destroy it in one orbit."

"Your engineer worries needlessly," Trahnee said. "Come with me, Pier. I'll show you how our defensive shield works." The tall, dark woman paused for a moment, then added, "Your engineer can accompany us, also, if she chooses."

"Tia?" Norlin didn't know what to say. The woman's engineering expertise might come in handy. She saw details he didn't, both because of her training and from her years of experience aboard battle-class vessels. He knew this, yet he wanted her to remain behind—because he had to be alone with Trahnee.

"I want to contact the *Preceptor*, Cap'n." She glanced at the control board where Bo Delamier sat idly playing with the instruments. "I'd like to look over this end of the system, too."

"Do that," Trahnee said. She took Norlin's arm and guided him from the office before he could protest. "This way, Pier. See how well we have done with such primitive resources?"

Norlin found it hard to concentrate on the decorations when he was with the genhanced woman. She had a quality about her that attracted him more and more. She wasn't beautiful—it was something more, and less, than symmetrical features or fine bone structure.

"You're not paying attention," she chided.

"Sorry. I'm not interested in how you turned the station into a replica of the emperor's court. We're still in danger. The Death Fleet is overpowering."

"You worry so, Pier. That can become tedious. Trust us. Bo and I know what we're doing. Here," she said, "look this over. It might put your mind to rest about our capacity to defend the Renfro mines and this space station."

"I don't understand," he said after looking over the diagrams she had summoned to a small vidscreen for him. "These aren't fighting mirrors, yet they function like them."

"Those are robot satellites. Bo programmed them to obey his signal. Each fights independently or in concert with the others. It's a complicated system that integrates all knowledge obtained from any source."

"One station knows what another is doing? How is that any different from a standard c-in-c?"

"Each satellite knows everything the others know and acts accordingly. It was very expensive to build, but what else is there to do out here? Of course, there is far more to it than that. The individual satellites evaluate their battle conditions and adjust constantly. If one decides it cannot destroy a target, others help."

"It maximizes destruction and minimizes energy expenditure?" Norlin asked. "Even so..."

"We have a combination of lasartillery, missiles and... other weapons."

"What else?"

"Don't be such a drudge, Pier. You must take time off to relax. That's as important as work, you know."

"The Death Fleet—" His words were cut off when three others came into the room.

"There you are!" cried Trahnee, obviously pleased at seeing her friends. "I thought you'd gone for a walk outside without your spacesuits."

The trio laughed in a way that put Norlin on his guard. From their erratic behavior and dilated pupils, he guessed that they were under the influence of powerful mood-altering drugs.

"They use them during combat. Don't worry," said Trahnee, answering his unspoken thought. "The drugs are all approved by Emperor Arian's court physicians. We can remain alert and at the peak of our considerable power for weeks, if required."

"Drugs exhaust you," Norlin said. "They'll let you down when you least expect it. It's better to use auto-med unit monitors to maintain alertness."

"Those silly little machines? They beep and annoy us so much. Genhanced people are very easily affected by extraneous input. Our senses are more acute, in addition to our intelligence and other abilities being greater."

"Then why do you have the sirens set at such a high level? My ears still ring from the combat warning."

"That?" Trahnee laughed lightly. Norlin was reminded of bells chiming in a gentle breeze. "Bo insisted. Too many of us ignored less strident calls to duty. It *is* boring on this space station."

"Why do you stay if you find duty here so objectionable?"

Trahnee turned away and spoke softly to one of her friends. They laughed, and she looked back at Norlin as if she hadn't heard his question.

"The only thing that makes it bearable out on the fringes of civilization is having other genhanced stationed here. The entire station is manned by us, in fact."

"What about the miners down on Renfro?"

"Them? Hardly. Sometimes, I'm not sure they would qualify as belonging to the same species. Prehistoric beings, often. Only one or two rise above the poisonous muck they work in."

Norlin wondered how she viewed him. Hardly better than she did the miners, he decided. Life in the shadow of the Crystal Throne must be brighter than even the most radiant day on another world.

She motioned for him to sit. He sank into a chair comprised more of electricity than solid material. Norlin floated just centimeters above the deck. The chair tingled wherever its field touched him. As uneasy as he was when he sat, the effect soon soothed him and relaxed tensed muscles. Even his hand stopped throbbing when he laid it on a charge-misty arm.

"You like this?" Trahnee asked.

"Very much. I've never seen anything like it before. Is it something you brought from Earth?"

"Hardly," she said. "Bo invented it. He is very clever when it comes to such gadgets. The space station is filled with them."

Norlin relaxed further, even though he knew he should tend to duty. Barse must have contacted the *Preceptor* by now. He had to know when the cruiser would rendezvous and pick them up. Even though Trahnee assured him the station's defensive system was impervious, he had experienced the full might of the Death Fleet, and they had not. Communicating the awesome power of the aliens proved difficult for him.

He hoped Delamier believed what was in the reports enough to prepare for the worst.

"Bo takes his duty seriously," she said. "So do they, even though you don't appreciate it." Trahnee pointed to the other three genhanced officers as they frolicked like small children, chasing each other around the room in a game of tag that didn't seem to have any rules. "This eases the responsibility and tedium of such a vital post."

"You don't believe that, do you?" Norlin said. "You're always sarcastic when you talk about the station. You don't have to stay in the Empire Service. You can do anything you want—this chair proves it."

"Bo did that. I have no talent in that vein. It doesn't matter, either. Such novelties would hardly support us in the manner to which we have become accustomed."

Norlin knew such furniture would be a sensation on any planet along the star frontier. On Earth, where the populace was richer and inclined to follow fads, it would prove even more popular. Something more lay behind the woman's words. No one got rich in the Empire Service on the salaries paid, even with combat pay. Trahnee had hinted she and Delamier stole from the rare earth shipments leaving the mines below. This made Norlin uncomfortable. His duty was clear in such a case, yet he didn't want to press the issue further. Sending Trahnee and Delamier to Earth for trial before Emperor Arian ranked low on his list of priorities. None of them might survive the coming alien attack.

"What do *you* think about the aliens?" he asked. "We included a physiological workup in our report."

"Scrawny insects," sniffed Trahnee. "Arachnoids, actually, from the photos. Their physique is hardly important. How they use it and how they think are the important points. You neglected this aspect completely."

"What can you tell me about their psychology? What would cause them to surrender?" Norlin put into words something that had bothered him from his very first sighting of the alien Death Fleet. "What causes them to plunder like they do without even trying to contact us?"

"You are single-minded, aren't you? All you can talk about are those spindly bugs."

"Trahnee," he said earnestly, "they are deadly. You've seen our reports. Look over our battle data. Their smallest scout ships give the *Preceptor* a hard fight."

She sniffed. "Even this Captain Pensky, small as his abilities were, proved that they can be defeated."

Norlin nodded. Pensky had been a genhanced officer; he had also thought the aliens' ability to be negligible.

"We..." he began. From the corner of his eye, he saw Barse motioning to him. "A moment."

He left the woven-electricity chair with some reluctance. Its current surging through his tired muscles had invigorated him and erased much of the pain he felt. His right arm had returned to normal during the few seconds he had spent there.

"Cap'n, we picked 'em up again. A small fleet segment. About a dozen of the heavy planet beamers."

"So few?"

"They must know this is a mining planet. They might also know its atmosphere doesn't support our life form."

"The yttrium mined below might be important to them, though."

"They've tried their usual tactics," his engineer pointed out. "We don't have the capability to hold 'em off for long. I've checked."

"What of our ship?"

"Still out of position, still looking at a major battle just to redock. Cap'n, I don't say things like this lightly, but I think we're all history. The aliens have us by the—"

Sirens went off. Norlin clamped his hands over his ears, then shook off the strident effects. A subsonic note drove straight through to the center of his brain. He wondered if the genhanced needed this extra prod to bring them out of their drug-induced haze. Most of those lounging about had stirred and now moved sluggishly toward their battle stations.

Genhanced or not, they had no chance against even a minor segment of the Death Fleet.

"Let's do what we can. If we create enough of a ruckus, we can keep them from going after the *Preceptor*," he said, thoughts entirely on his ship. He cursed the bad luck that separated him from his command.

"Oh, Pier, you show no confidence in us. We can defeat those bugs." Trahnee took his arm and reached for Tia Barse's. The engineer shied away as if the woman's touch was toxic. Norlin started to object, too, then the words faded on his lips. Being so close to Trahnee made him feel good. He didn't even try to analyze the sensation. She was a lovely woman, in a stark, angular way.

"How do you intend to defeat such heavily armed vessels?" asked Barse. "Bore them to death?"

Trahnee ignored the engineer's sarcastic comment. "Come this way. We can watch them be blown from space."

"The relay system you used before won't work. They learn from their mistakes," warned Norlin.

"We have other methods. More devious ones," she said with a confidence he wished he shared.

They settled into comfortable seats near the command center. Bo Delamier worked expertly at his control console. Norlin tried to figure out what the genhanced officer did. When he couldn't, he turned to Barse. She shook her head. It made no sense to her, either.

"He's burning up a lot of energy for nothing much that I can see, Cap'n. We'd better check out their combat escape system."

"That won't be necessary," Trahnee assured them. "Watch. We won't even use the energy transfer system."

The immense vidscreen dominating the command center showed small dots moving slowly around the disc of Renfro II. The planet shielded a half-dozen other alien warships. Any of the huge planet beamers could destroy this pitiful space station with a single application of the devastating rainbow-hued energy weapon. Delamier seemed oblivious to the fact as he continued to work diligently.

Just as Norlin started to ask what the man had done, he leaned back, a satisfied smile curling his thin lips. Delamier turned and gave a thumbs-up to Trahnee.

"We are fully defended," she said.

"Cap'n, look!" Barse leaned forward in her chair, eyes wide as she stared at the vidscreen.

A hundred battleships winked into view at precise points around the space station. Norlin's expert gaze identified those points as the most advantageous for defending the station from attack.

"He is a genius. There is no one quite like Bo," Trahnee declared with some satisfaction. But she looked at Norlin, not at Delamier as she spoke.

"Those aren't real," Norlin said suddenly. "They're holographic projections. He's trying to bluff the aliens into thinking a major fleet element surrounds us!"

"It won't work," Barse said. "They're smarter than that. Spectro readings. Gravimetric readings. Even radiation levels will show there's nothing there."

"Oh?" Trahnee raised a well-plucked eyebrow in a superior manner.

"They're turning from the attack," Norlin said in awe. "They're leaving orbit without firing a shot."

"Isn't that the essence of warfare? To win without casualties?" she asked.

He watched as the tiny portion of the Death Fleet left orbit and jetted for deep space. Bo Delamier had used a clever trick and won—for the moment. How long would it be before the aliens returned with forces large enough to overwhelm even a hundred human battleships?

Chapter Five

"Are you impressed with my easy victory, Captain Norlin?" asked Bo Delamier.

"They've left for the time being. When they return, this station will be turned into metal and carbon vapor. They didn't think they could defeat you with a few ships. They know they can with a thousand—or more."

"You have no idea what you're saying, Norlin," the space station commander said acidly. "If they ever dare to return—and I doubt those rebels ever will—we'll simply show them even bigger ships, even more of a challenge to overcome. They will leave us alone then. I know their kind."

"Have you worked this…scam before?" asked Tia Barse.

"I'd call it a clever tactic, not a scam," Delamier said diffidently. "However, it has proven effective in other circumstances."

"Where?" pressed Barse.

"Let's just say we have had call to use it," cut in Trahnee. "It has worked well enough that Emperor Arian gave Bo a commendation for it."

"It works once," said Norlin. "And then only if the enemy is overly cautious. What if the aliens had thrown their planet beamers against your holographic projections?"

"The space station's batteries are sufficient to take out their vessels," Delamier said. "It would appear as if the battleships had done the deed. That would keep any enemy away from us. I'm sure they will shift for another system and leave us alone now. They are, after all, only cowardly rebels."

"You don't know them, even if you *have* read my reports," said Norlin. "They're *aliens*, and they're looking for something on the worlds they loot. If we could figure out what it is they're willing to murder entire worlds for, we might be able to stop them before they devastate any more of our planets."

"That's of no real concern," Delamier said. "The emperor entrusted the Renfro system to me. I have performed my task admirably. Who cares about other colonial worlds?"

"The Empire Service is charged with protecting them, as well as Earth and the Inner Worlds," snapped Norlin, angered by the genhanced officer's attitude. "You're in the Service, too. Simply diverting the Death Fleet isn't the answer."

"Getting killed by them isn't, either," pointed out Trahnee. "Oh, come now, you two should not argue like that. We ought to be friends."

Norlin and Delamier started to protest, but neither found it in himself to continue after Trahnee bade them stop. Norlin wanted only to be with her and listen to her soft, soothing voice. He thought he might explain the importance of the *Preceptor*'s mission to her, since Delamier was a lost cause. Nothing would penetrate the genhanced officer's shield of arrogance and egotism.

"Cap'n, let's contact our ship and get the hell out of here," said Barse. "We'll be in trouble up to our asteroids when the real Death Fleet gets here."

Vexed at the engineer's words, Trahnee licked her lips and started to speak. Norlin cut her off.

"She's right. We have to go. Now." His words provoked Trahnee even more. A look of stark disbelief flashed across her face, then vanished as suddenly as it had appeared.

"If you desire. Bo, contact their ship."

"I've tried," the space station commander said irritably. "They're under com blackout. All I can do is broadcast and wait for a laser com-link from them."

"You can't detect the *Preceptor*?" demanded Norlin. He felt as if he had been dropped into zero-g. The station had equipment adequate to find his ship, no matter how the cruiser tried to block transmission. Emergency bands, classified detector frequencies that changed billions of times a second to provide absolute identification, other techniques that should have pinpointed the ship.

"Cap'n, that means the *Preceptor*'s been destroyed."

He looked at Barse. He tried to speak, but words wouldn't come.

"Oh, don't be so negative," said Trahnee. "There are reasons why we can't find them. Not all our staff are as clever as Bo about these things."

"Commander Delamier?" asked Norlin. "Have you *personally* tried to contact the *Preceptor*?"

"They weren't destroyed," the genhanced man said, clearly not wanting to pursue the topic further. "We didn't get any Dirac delta function energy spike indication, as if they had blown up or plunged into the atmosphere."

"The radiation cannon might have masked it," said Barse.

"Stop outgassing about this 'alien death fleet' and 'radiation cannon' and all the rest," ordered Delamier. "They've left orbit—and abandoned you. They're cowards. They all are. None can stand against my might."

He stormed off. Trahnee looked from Norlin to Delamier, as if torn. She came to a quick decision and followed the genhanced officer, not even looking back as she hurried away.

"Let's find the escape tubes. We aren't going to be able to hitch a ride on the *Preceptor* when the Death Fleet returns in strength," Barse said.

Norlin nodded. The two went off in search of a computer terminal that afforded them access to space station diagrams. He worked for several minutes before pinpointing the small capsules that would be launched in case of damage to the station.

"They don't provide much coverage, do they, Cap'n? If you're not in the command center, you don't get away from this space station."

"Each tube has four capsules—and there are only two launchers," he said, finishing his survey. "They might list more under a classified heading."

"Why bother?" asked Barse. "Evac drills are supposed to be held every ten days. You don't keep evacuation tubes a secret from your staff, unless you intend to lose most of them."

Norlin leaned back in the hard chair and tried to think like the genhanced officer. He saw no reason to classify such a basic life-support unit.

"He doesn't think he'll ever need to use it," he decided. "He's diverted money allocated to establish the system to other projects. Perhaps the holographic ships, perhaps the computer-driven defensive system. Who knows what else he has actually built? I would certainly like to know what other weapon he used to destroy the scouts around the planet, also." He considered trying to access the computer onboard the station but knew the commander would have it under top secret lock and key.

"I know I want to be sitting in a capsule and ready to fly," said Barse. "Inside the escape egg, we're easy targets for a sweep with a radiation cannon, but it looks to be a better risk than staying with the space station. These fools are going to be blown to space dust when the aliens return because they don't believe there is any danger at all."

Norlin agreed. "I want to check the deep-space detectors. Even though the alien scouts replaced their sensors—Delamier still won't admit it—we might be able to glean some small tidbit from them."

"We can hunt for the *Preceptor*, too," Barse said. She swallowed hard. The stolid, normally stony-face woman showed a flash of emotion as she added, "Or the debris."

Norlin and Barse entered the command center. Most of the genhanced officers once more lounged about, joking with one another, sharing their drugs and neglecting their duty. One sat in the corner and ran his fingers in intricate patterns along the wall, trying to perform complex mathematical equations without benefit of leaving greasy smears on anything.

Norlin sat down at a sensor console and began running through the readouts. He sagged when he saw he had been right and Delamier wrong.

He hit the alarm and projected his readings onto the vidscreen for everyone to see. "The Death Fleet is on its way back. Eighteen hundred ships, by my count," he announced.

He glanced over his shoulder and saw Delamier's surprised look. The surprise turned to anger. The commander stalked to his console and began working to project thousands of ships around the space station.

Norlin saw immediately that it wouldn't work. The advance element of the alien fleet formed into a huge ring with its weaponry aimed inward toward the axis. They would pass by, Renfro II and its defending space station sucked into the maw, the Death Fleet's potent radiation cannon aimed into the center. Any structure caught inside would be reduced to radioactive slag within microseconds.

"Here, Cap'n," came Barse's urgent voice. She motioned from the far side of the command center. She pulled a bulkhead panel back to reveal the first of four escape capsules. Norlin checked the vidscreen once more and saw no hope of the space station surviving the Death Fleet's attack. Already he saw rainbow discharges around the muzzles of their radiation cannon, a sure indicator of intense energy release.

"Commander," he called, "your pretty pictures won't stop them this time. Neither will your computer-driven defensive system. Prepare to evacuate. I don't know that the escape paths will save very many of us, but we have to try to get away *now*."

The sirens blared again. Norlin cringed. He motioned to Trahnee, who looked unsure of herself for the first time since he'd come aboard the space station. Never had he seen a woman more appealing. Beauty rode with this one, he decided. And more, so much more. He wanted to go to her and pick her up and carry her to the escape pods. To stay much longer in the station courted death.

Trahnee spoke rapidly with Delamier. The space station commander looked frightened. He stared at the vidscreen and the impressive might arrayed against him. She tugged at his sleeve and continued to harangue him. Like a man robbed of volition, he followed her.

"What about the others?" asked Barse, looking around the command center. "Aren't you allowing them to evacuate, too?"

Trahnee pushed Delamier in front of her. He got into the escape capsule, staring ahead fixedly, as if he had gone into shock.

"They'll be all right," she said. "They are genhanced. They know what to do to survive."

Norlin didn't argue with her. He wasn't going to allow the space station staff to die without giving them a fair chance.

The station lacked enough escape tubes for many to flee. He touched the GENERAL QUARTERS alarm and the EVACUATION button simultaneously. A few in the command center stood and stared at the open panel as if unsure of themselves. Norlin wondered if they had ever gone through an evacuation exercise before. It now meant their deaths that they didn't know what to do.

He had done all he could. He crowded in behind Barse and touched the button to seal the capsule. The four of them were plunged into absolute darkness. Delamier let out a tiny squeak of fear. Trahnee soothed him immediately, her voice like honey flowing through the Stygian gloom. Thick, padded bands snapped from the arms and back of the seats, cushioning them against rapid, violent maneuvering.

A clock ticked off ten seconds. At the tenth click, the capsule blasted from the space station. Norlin almost blacked out from the powerful acceleration. He thanked the hours of training he had endured at the Empire Service Academy. He wasn't sure what benefit he got from being able to watch the tiny vidscreen in front of him as Renfro's planetary disk surged toward him, but he at least knew he was still alive. For the moment.

Readouts from the limited sensory equipment aboard the capsule showed high levels of radiation all around. It might be from the Death Fleet's cannon, or it might be that they were going through the planets van Allen radiation belt. He couldn't tell. Abrupt changes in the thrust vector kept him from thinking clearly or finding the proper combination of instruments that would tell the space station's fate.

"We're going in hard, Cap'n," Tia Barse said morosely. "I hate planets. Why do we always have to walk with all the gravity pulling us down?"

The scream of the thick methane-and-ammonia atmosphere against the egg's hull drowned out the rest of her words. From the two genhanced he heard nothing. He hoped they had survived the violent maneuvering. The buffeting had been bad as the capsule randomly dodged about to avoid attack, and their radiation exposure had pushed their biologicals to the limit. Now, the vibration rattled his teeth and threatened to rip apart their escape capsule.

Norlin began to worry when their descent lingered on past a few minutes. Whiffs of methane entered the capsule and sent his pulse pounding as he began to cough and choke. If the shell had been cracked, they might die long before they landed.

They might die even *if* they landed. He hadn't had time to check the survival gear aboard before they evacuated. Unless they had an ample number of spacesuits, they were trapped in the leaking capsule. No one held their breath on a ten-bar pressure-wracked world.

Even as he worried, the capsule crashed to the ground and skidded for kilometers. The impact rattled him again. It took several minutes for him to regain his senses after the capsule stopped skipping along the surface of the planet. Even so, he was the first to recover.

Tia Barse hung limp and unmoving in her harnesses. He reached over and pressed a life-audit tab. It winked green. He heaved a sigh of relief. She was unconscious but alive. He couldn't reach forward to either Trahnee or Delamier.

"Report," he called. He choked on the methane leaking into the capsule, rubbed his watering eyes and tried not to breathe too deeply. "Are you alive?"

"How inane," came Trahnee's indolent voice. "If we had perished during your clumsy landing, would we be speaking now? Or do you believe in ghosts?"

"Landing was automatic," he said, not wanting to argue. "We've got to get into spacesuits fast. We're taking on poisonous atmosphere. With ten times Earth-normal pressure, even a tiny crack will turn into a jet in a few minutes."

"Are there suits aboard?" the genhanced woman asked. "We always thought that a radio beacon would be enough for the miners to home in on and rescue us if we ever had to land in these silly craft."

Norlin cursed. If they lacked even one spacesuit, someone died. If they didn't have any suits, they were all candidates for high-pressure methane decomposition within a few minutes.

"Cap'n?" came Barse's weak voice. She sat up and strained against the restraining harness. Irritated, she pushed it away. "We've got to get into suits. High pressure leaks—"

"I know," he told her, cutting off a full report. "I don't know if we have any spacesuits."

"All models of this escape egg do," Barse said. She worked under the tiny instrument panel. A loud *click!* sounded, and parts of the wall fell away to either side. "They use the suits for added exterior protection. Not a good scheme if we took any direct hits but adequate for non-combat situations."

Norlin grabbed his flimsy nano-material spacesuit and began testing it. All seams and sides held pressure. He awkwardly began donning the suit, moving painfully in the tight compartment.

"Get into your suits," he ordered the others. "We don't have much time." A single red light blinked slowly on his simple instrument panel showing corruption of internal atmosphere. When the light shone a steady red, they'd have less than five minutes to live.

Norlin sealed his touch-seams and adjusted oxygen mixture flow to the lowest possible level. Conservation now might mean life later.

"Where's the laser beacon?" demanded Bo Delamier. The genhanced officer had finally shaken off the shock and now tried to reassert himself.

"Can we reach the miners on-planet?" asked Norlin. "Trying to signal the space station now might bring the aliens down on top of us, if there's even a station left, and I doubt there is. They're thorough. They don't let even a blade of grass survive once they begin their attack."

"Are you implying we're like some lower life form to them?" asked Trahnee. The question was couched in surprise and outrage. "But we're genhanced!"

"We haven't had much chance to debate the point with them, since we've so busy killing each other," Norlin said dryly. He studied the instruments and found that nothing worked. The idiot light showing atmospheric quality had turned a bright red. The air inside the capsule was deadly now, and had corroded all their instruments.

"What else do we have in the way of equipment?" he asked Barse.

"An inertial compass," she answered, "but it doesn't do us any good since it hasn't been set. We can find our way back to the capsule if we wander off, but not much else. There won't be any global positioning satellites orbiting around the planet, not if the aliens do their usual thorough job of destruction."

"Delamier, can you pinpoint our crash site? We need to know how far it is to any human outpost."

"There's only one," Trahnee said. "Upper continent, by a large ammonia ocean."

As she spoke, Norlin knew survival would be even harder for them than he'd thought. The atmospheric content hadn't triggered other warnings it should have. For methane and ammonia to exist as they did on this stony world required more than high pressure—it required intense cold. He wondered how any deposit of rare earths had ever come to this failed gas giant.

"Insulators on your boots," he ordered. "If you can find them, double up. We need to keep from getting frostbite. Then we're going to explore. I don't want to stay in the capsule longer than necessary. It must leave a heat signature bright enough for a blind man to find."

"Then the miners can locate us easily enough," Trahnee said brightly.

"So can the aliens. They only need to look down from orbit with an infrared detector, and we'll stand out on the cold landscape."

"Oh," she said, chagrined at not having thought of this.

"Where are we going?" asked Delamier. "One spot on this empire-damned planet is like another."

"We've got to believe the capsule's programming was sophisticated enough to take us toward other humans. If we aren't even on the same continent, we're dead."

"I refuse to die like this," said Delamier. "Let's go find the miners. They're around somewhere. I'm sure of it."

"Is that your genhanced mentality talking or just fear?" goaded Barse.

Norlin waved her to silence. They had enough problems facing them without arguing.

He checked to be sure everyone's spacesuit was properly sealed, much to the genhanced couple's chagrin, then he opened the hatch. The gust of methane wind coming in staggered him, pinning him in his seat. He recovered, grabbed the hatch frame, pulled himself forward and looked around outside.

"What's that?" he asked, peering through the swirling murk. He used a handheld light to show the spot he meant.

"It's a land roamer," cried Barse. "I'd recognize it anywhere! We must be near the outpost!"

"I'm not picking up any chatter on the radio," Norlin said. "All I hear is static. The aliens must have killed everyone on-planet by now."

"Don't be ridiculous. That's only natural interference," said Delamier. "Heavy storm activity makes radio transmission difficult. We'll have to rely on an x-ray com laser to reach the station. The emergency beacons are configured for a methane-ammonia window far outside the visible spectrum."

The genhanced space station commander hefted a beacon and stepped outside. The gusty winds of deadly gas caused him to totter.

"Don't," cautioned Norlin. "Let's try to find the miners' outpost first. Then we can see what's happened to the station."

"Your so-called aliens haven't destroyed it," Delamier said confidently. "They don't have the firepower. They're only aliens, after all."

Norlin and Barse lashed themselves together and fought the high winds to examine the land roamer. The closer they got, the more Norlin's heart sank.

"Abandoned," said Barse, putting into words what he had feared most. "It broke down, and they didn't even try to repair it."

"What's wrong with it?" asked Trahnee.

"Who knows? Most of the drive train and engine compartment are sealed against the atmosphere. It'd take special equipment to crack 'em open to check."

Norlin slipped into the cockpit and rummaged around. A smile spread on his lips. He held up a flimsy sheet of plastic.

"A map!" he called. "With coordinates. We should be able to locate our crash site and use the inertial compass to find the outpost."

"That's not necessary," said Delamier. "They've found us already. I knew the miners wouldn't let us rot out here out here in this poisonous atmosphere for long."

Norlin and Barse whipped around, eyes scanning the thick overcast. Polarizers in their face-plates reacted to cut out the brilliant flares of landing jets.

"They've found us," Trahnee squealed with uncharacteristic glee.

"That they have," Norlin said, having seen such mechanisms before on Sutton II. "But it's not the miners. Those are the alien ground fighting machines. We don't stand a chance against them!"

Chapter Six

Don't be ridiculous…" Bo Delamier began. He stood and stared when a second flare blazed through the swirling murky atmosphere. Dozens more came, until the sky lit up brighter than any Earth day. Even Delamier could no longer argue this was a simple rescue party.

"They've locked onto us," said Barse. "I picked up a modulated wave a few seconds ago."

"They've locked onto the capsule, not us," Norlin said. He studied the plastic map again, trying to make sense from it. "The outpost is less than ten kilometers off, if my estimate of our location is right."

"Ten klicks or ten light-years, what's the difference?" asked Barse.

"We're close to an automated mine. It must be over in that direction." He pointed, ignoring his engineer's pessimistic comment. "Not far, either. Less than a kilometer."

"Less than *that*," came Trahnee's voice. She had wandered off through the swirling methane and dust. "I found an airlock only a hundred meters away. The counter shows human miners descended less than an hour ago."

"An hour? We're saved!" cried Delamier.

"The hell we are," said Barse.

The brightness in the air faded slowly. The last of the alien fighting machines had landed. Each pod carried five of the deadly robot tanks, but only one of the five sported a living alien to guide the others. Norlin had fought them on Sutton and respected their toughness. Even if the alien died, the robots fought on with almost perfect coordination of effort with other alien weapons.

"Abandon the egg. Let's get down into the mine," he ordered. "I don't want to be above-ground when they open fire. We can't see very far in this methane fog and would make easy targets."

Even as he spoke, a huge gout of flame lanced through the murky atmosphere and bathed the escape capsule. The tough shell resisted for several seconds then exploded in a ball of fire.

"They sublimated the carbon composite hull!" exclaimed Delamier. "That's not possible unless they're using a plasma torch."

"Who cares what they're using?" asked Barse. "Those weapons are enough to toast us to a turn if we stick our pretty necks in front of them."

Norlin found Trahnee in the swirling murk and pushed her aside. He checked the time clock on the airlock she had led them to and saw that she had accurately reported. Humans had entered this mine shaft only an hour before. They might have been the ones who had abandoned the land roamer. They still might even be in touch with the human outpost.

"Inside," he ordered. "Now! We've got to find them and warn the others—"

The roar from the approaching alien tanks drowned out his words. He turned up the volume of his speaker and repeated the command. Barse and Trahnee obeyed. Delamier seemed paralyzed—or hypnotized. He stood and stared at the approaching mechanized death.

"Get down the shaft. I'll get him," he told Trahnee. She started to protest, but Barse grabbed her by the arm and wheeled her around. Norlin regretted his decision instantly.

He stared down the muzzle of an immensely powerful radiation cannon. He saw the tiny sparks deep inside its lasing chamber as a charge built. He wasted no time imagining what it would be like if the robot mechanism fired at such close range—he knew the destruction it had brought to Sutton from hundreds of kilometers into space.

It would be no less frightful here.

"Delamier! Bo!" He dived parallel to the ground. His shoulder struck the genhanced officer behind the knees and snapped Delamier backward as if the cannon had fired and mowed him down. Delamier fought for an instant then stopped, rolled over and sat up, still staring mutely at the robot tank.

"It's big," Norlin said softly.

He turned down the amplification when he heard feedback starting. Delamier continued to stare—and it wasn't fear that paralyzed him. Norlin saw madness lurking in those wide blue eyes.

"We don't have to watch. We can go. We can leave it behind." His own nerves began to betray him. He glanced constantly from the seated officer to the monster tank lumbering inexorably forward. It didn't have to discharge its cannon to kill; its bulk could crush, too.

Norlin shrieked and hit Delamier with his shoulder. The pair of them rolled to one side as the radiation cannon fired. A huge gout of dirt and rock rocketed skyward, vanishing into the swirling clouds of ammonia and methane overhead. The heat stifled Norlin, even in his efficient heat-radiating spacesuit. He shivered when he saw the warning strips inside his suit turn black—even though he had avoided the main beam, he had just sustained a lethal amount of radiation. If he failed to receive treatment within the hour, he would die.

Already, he imagined his mouth turning dry and his gums bleeding until his mouth filled. Skin flaked off. His vision blurred. He died from a radiation overdose.

He didn't even have an hour.

"In, you fool," came Delamier's angry voice. "You want to get us killed?"

Strong hands lifted Norlin and dragged him to the mineshaft. The door cycled open, allowing them to tumble into the airlock. Norlin struggled to get his feet under him. He failed. All he could see were the burnt-black warning strips inside his spacesuit.

The lift dropped them a hundred meters before he regained his senses. From above, he heard a deep-throated rumble and knew the robot tank had destroyed the airlock so that dangerous atmospheric gas flooded the mine. He hoped the mine's leak detectors worked efficiently enough to warn the humans already below.

"The cage and its mechanism—what will happen to it with the airlock gone?" he asked Delamier.

"It's a magnetic railcar. We can run wherever there are tracks still intact." Delamier sounded more in control, so Norlin forced himself to calmness. It wouldn't do to have the genhanced taking command.

Norlin studied Delamier and saw no hint of the madness that had held him in thrall only minutes earlier. Knees threatening to buckle, Norlin stood upright. He took several deep, steadying breaths and almost fainted because he had set the oxygen level too low in the spacesuit for such heavy breathing.

"Where is she? Where did Trahnee go?" demanded Delamier.

"They entered ahead of us. I have no idea how far down into the shaft they went already," Norlin said. "I promised her I'd save you."

"I didn't need saving," Delamier said, sneering. "I am invincible!"

"You just lost your command. The Death Fleet has destroyed the space station and its entire crew by now."

"I doubt that. This is unnecessary. My defenses worked perfectly. They had to. I designed them." The genhanced officer refused to admit what he had seen with his own eyes. The aliens were in complete control of Renfro II and had undoubtedly destroyed the space station without much effort.

"Barse?" called Norlin. He waited for a reply. A faint interference hiss turned into a binary coded message in his earpiece. His engineer feared the aliens and their ability to tap into human com-links.

He stopped the car, got a bearing and told Delamier, "That way. Five hundred meters. They're in a stope waiting for us."

"You claim telepathy as a skill, too?" Delamier's sneer was open now. "I received no such message nor do I see evidence that anyone traveled in that direction."

"Then stay here." Norlin had no more time for the genhanced officer. He had promised Trahnee he wouldn't leave him on the surface. He had rescued him, in spite of Delamier's shock and fear at seeing the alien fighting machines. He hadn't said he would deliver the officer to her once they got to the relative safety afforded by the underground tunnels.

He walked off. He didn't have to turn around to know Delamier followed a few paces behind. Faint vibrations through the laser-chewed stone floor told him. Norlin tried not to smile at this minor victory.

He stopped when he heard a long burst of static. Five meters away in a sloping stope sat Barse and Trahnee.

"They took out the airlock," he said. "What else have you detected?"

"Keep your power levels low, Cap'n. I detected alien entry into the mine. They can track our radio emissions."

"What nonsense," blurted Delamier. "You talk about those machines as if they had a will of their own. The Emperor forbade such machines a century ago. Which ones have aliens in them as controllers? We kill them, and the other robots run down."

"It's not that easy. They're all linked, perhaps like you had your satellite defensive system coordinated. One helps the other if it runs into trouble. They don't need the alien intelligence to guide them, either. They operate autonomously."

"It's more than an expert system," Barse concluded for her captain. "They've pushed artificial intelligence to incredible levels, the Emperor be damned."

"Ridiculous," scoffed Delamier. "Where are the miners? We can get weapons from them. They must have something we can use to destroy the aliens." He shoved his thumb toward the surface.

"I detected three miners farther down, Cap'n," said Barse. "Do you want me to get them?"

"Do so. The aliens won't be content with remaining on the surface. They'll come after us. Scrubbing all life from a world is as important to them as looting it." Norlin said nothing about needing medical attention. He felt stronger but knew the radiation gnawed away at his cells, destroying and permanently altering. He needed an auto-med's full service or he would die—within a very short time now.

"Paranoid delusions," Delamier declared. "Are all mere humans so crazed?"

Norlin almost blurted out how it was the genhanced who were crazy. He held back when he saw Trahnee's expression behind her clear face-plate.

That she appealed to him barely covered the facts. He wanted her. She was the most beautiful woman he had ever seen and he wanted her. Now.

"You folks. What're you doing here? What's going on upstairs?" came the crackling radio transmission. Norlin jerked away from Trahnee's intense gray eyes to see a trio of miners waddling toward him. They were outfitted in heavy suits designed for work in this dangerous environment. Equipment he failed to identify swung at their belts. He couldn't make out their faces behind the heavy glasteel visors shielding their faces, but he guessed they were all frowning.

"Captain Norlin, Empire Service Cruiser *Preceptor*," he said briskly. "This is Commander Delamier from the space station. The entire planet is under siege by alien invaders."

"What's this space dust?" demanded one of the faceless three. "We got no warning."

"The Death Fleet destroyed the station before a warning could be sent out," said Barse.

"Death Fleet? This is one of your genhanced games, isn't it? We don't appreciate it, Delamier. You can take it and—" The man's voice cut off. Norlin heard crosstalk from a different frequency and knew the warning had finally been relayed from the on-planet headquarters.

"You may be an empire lackey but you weren't kidding," another said. "We *are* under attack by aliens."

"My defenses are adequate to contain and destroy them," Delamier said.

"Then get your damned defenses working. The space station is dust, as is the satellite system you deployed around Renfro. We're it, Delamier. We are all that's left in the system," the first miner said.

"Cap'n, I'm picking up sideband messages. They're in the mines," warned Barse.

"Where can we hide?" asked Norlin. "We'll have to find a place to make a stand."

"What are we going to use for weapons?" demanded Delamier. "We can't hit them with rocks!"

"Why not?" asked one miner. "We lure the aliens into a shaft and collapse it. Simple."

Norlin doubted it. Any fighting machine sent underground would be able to burrow. Even a collapsing mineshaft might not stop the pursuing juggernauts.

"How? Explosives?" he asked. "We might use the explosives directly against the robots."

"Robots? That's all we're dealing with?" A miner shook his head. Norlin saw the man's entire body quake as if he laughed silently. He didn't want to argue with him about the seriousness of pursuit by the Death Fleet's ground fighting machines.

"This way," another said. "They'll have to come down the main shaft, unless they're tunneling on their own. The strain gauges we've placed around don't show that happening."

The trio of miners led them down the tunnel into a small rock chamber hardly large enough for all of them. Here the miners had established a temporary command center. Small readouts showed the progress of a dozen or more rock chewers. In spite of himself, Norlin studied the instruments and evaluated the progress of the mining robots. He was impressed by their output.

"We can use a chewer to plant the blow," a miner said. "Lure them into a stope and kerpow them!"

From the corner of his eye, Norlin saw Delamier working with a small box near the instrumentation power feeds. He started to ask the genhanced officer what he was doing when Trahnee touched his arm. The contact caused voltage to surge through his entire body, as if he had been electrocuted.

"We must do as Bo directs," she said softly. "For all our own sakes, I beg you to do everything he says."

"All right," Norlin agreed before he realized the words had slipped from his lips.

"We need a place to hide," Delamier said loudly. "Where can we go? Down?"

"Go up a level," a miner said. "There's an emergency shaft there. We'll join you in a few minutes. It'll take all three of us to position the chewers."

Norlin motioned to Barse to leave. He followed, Trahnee and Delamier following closely.

"This isn't working out right, Cap'n," Barse said. "My readouts show the aliens are almost on top of us. They must be ready to drill down and attack from above. Nothing else makes sense. That means we're going right into the jaws of their attack."

"The miners are the experts. Let them—"

An explosion rocked the mines and drove him to his knees. The tunnel filled with cloaking dust, and the shock wave deafened him momentarily. He wished he wore the heavier suit the miners used. Sound transmission from the outside wouldn't be as great.

"What happened?" he called out too loudly, partially deafened by the blast.

Delamier and Trahnee came up. Delamier pulled Norlin to his feet.

"What do you think, fool? I destroyed the alien robots hunting us down."

"How?" he asked numbly.

"Those fool miners were attracting them with their power emanations. Your engineer said they hunted by energy leakage, so I rigged a bomb to blow when the robots found it."

"The miners are dead?" Norlin asked, stunned.

"Of course they are. Without them as bait, the robots would never have been lured into the chamber," Delamier said smugly. "You overestimated their AI ability. They weren't anything more than the usual attack robots. The Emperor uses more complex units for his own amusement in the palace."

Norlin spun on the genhanced officer and slammed him hard against a rock wall. "You sacrificed three men!"

"What does it matter? They weren't genhanced," Delamier said, as if this explained everything.

Norlin almost killed him. If his engineer hadn't held him back, he would have overcome his growing weakness and done so.

Even worse than Delamier's casual destruction of three humans was the knowledge that the aliens hadn't been stopped. It took more than a single bomb blast to deter them.

That Pier Norlin knew for a fact.

Chapter Seven

Mitri Sarov grunted as his strong stubby fingers danced across the weapons computer. The program worked well. He nodded when he saw the statistical comparison? between perfection and actual performance. Again he had achieved a point-ninety-five correlation between his theoretical projection and reality.

"Chikako," he said into his throat microphone, making the small flexible strip tremble against his heavy flesh, "I need data on positions. Where are they?"

"The two scouts vectoring in on us have vanished," came the immediate reply in his left ear.

From on his right side came Gowan Liottey's grating, whining voice. "Mitri, I'm supposed to be in charge. I'm the ranking officer aboard this ship."

Sarov touched a button on his panel and checked the most recent auto-med report on the first officer. Liottey had improved under continual medical support, but the robotic doctor refused to give him an unconditional release. The extent of the CoolinGas damage to his brain remained to be mapped and repaired. Even if the auto-med cleared him medically, Liottey's erratic behavior endangered the *Preceptor* to the point that the stolid tac officer refused to relinquish control.

"It's logged that you're medically unfit, Gowan," he said. "Now, leave me alone. I have a battle to fight."

"Mitri!" protested Liottey. "I am filing an exception to your horrible, demeaning order. You can't imprison me like this. I demand to be given my command!"

"File the exception. The log is open to you, as it is to everyone on board. I'm recording the full battle, so the log might react sluggishly when you speak." Sarov savagely cut the connection, then said to Miza, "Don't let him through again. He's giving me a headache. Damn, but he whines worse than a turbine with a bent blade!"

"I wish the captain and Tia were here," the com officer said. Her fingers flew over the computer console controlling her communications links, doing by instinct what the automated sensors woven into her scalplock failed to do quickly enough. She monitored the progress of the Death Fleet—and the warships tracking them.

"They aren't here. Where are the damned aliens?" Sarov grumbled and growled, causing feedback from his throat mike. He stopped subvocalizing and put the data Chikako gave him on a tactical vidscreen.

The man's immensely strong fingers tapped on the edge of his console. As a tactical maneuver took form in his mind, he was unaware that he now gripped the metal edge and had bent it out of shape. His muddy brown eyes flashed from readouts on his heads-up display to the vidscreen where he tried several different maneuvers theoretically before ordering the ship's nav computer to duplicate them.

"We're in big trouble," he told Chikako.

The woman spun around at her console, sensors blinking like small lightning discharges. She pulled her mike away and called across the control room, "We can't abandon them."

"We don't have any choice. We slowed and went into a higher orbit. We got away from the scouts, but we cannot speed up and regain the space station's orbit. The planet beamers are coming in and bringing the rest of the fleet with them."

"The station's lasartillery worked well during the first skirmish," she pointed out. "They might have more hidden weaponry than we think."

"This is a colony space station," scoffed Sarov. "We are the firepower for the Empire, not them."

Chikako's distant warning sensors buzzed. She relayed the information directly to Sarov's display.

"Damn, see what I mean? They're coming back in strength." His vidscreen lit with the array of Death Fleet ships returning from their rendezvous point in deep space.

"Mitri, the space station has something other than fighting in mind. Check the energy emission spectrum."

"Holograms?"

"That's my guess."

Sarov snorted in disgust. "They intend to chase off the Death Fleet with pictures? What fools. They must all be gen-hanced to conceive of such a vac-brained scheme."

"Norlin knows them too well and hinted at that possibility," the com officer said.

Sarov turned back to the mock battles being fought on his vidscreen. Even the immensely fast, sophisticated operations computer he used for his simulations balked at what he asked. The alien fleet triumphed with each variation he requested. He leaned back and vented a deep sigh that shook his body.

"We have no chance to win if we fight. We have to run."

"We can't leave Tia and the captain on the space station," protested Chikako.

"If we don't, we'll end up an expanding, rapidly cooling cloud of plasma," Sarov said. "The battle computer shows no way of fighting so many ships and winning."

"Even using the radiation cannon?"

"Chikako," Sarov said tiredly, "we don't dare fire it. Even if Tia was here to nursemaid it and keep the rest of our systems from blowing out, it's good for only one shot. We'd be dead in space for hours."

He idly touched the circuit that linked him with the navigational computer. They had to retreat. They had no other choice.

"Destroyer coming around the planet, low, fast and on an intercept course with the space station," called Chikako.

Sarov's readouts flared the instant the com officer spoke. His carefully chosen escape route vanished. The alien destroyer made a pass at the hologram-shrouded space station, its immense radiation cannon fired a single burst and the station vaporized.

"It's on an intercept course with us," said Chikako. "We've got to fight. We can't run. It's too fast—and it has position on us."

Sarov cursed as he worked on his computer console. His fingers flew like fat birds, touching here, nesting there for long seconds before fluttering on. Chikako's evaluation proved all too accurate. The alien warship used Renfro's gravity well as a slingshot, came around at speed, destroyed the station with little effort and hurled on at them. No amount of dodging would get the *Preceptor* out of danger.

"Prepare the radiation cannon. We'll have the one shot. They won't expect it."

"Mitri..."

Sarov ignored her. He had too much to do getting the captured alien weapon ready. Even with his link-up to the command and navigational computers, he was pushed to his limits, and almost blinded by the flashing lights in his heads-up display, no matter how he tried to dim them.

"Mitri, it's not fair!"

The words from behind caused him to spin, yanked from his intense concentration. Gowan Liottey stood there, a pouting expression on his pale, drawn face. His blue eyes welled with tears.

"Aren't you under medication?" asked Sarov, startled at the man's sudden appearance.

"I stopped it. They can't force me to take anything, since I'm the rightful commander of the *Preceptor*."

"You're sick. Sit down and let me work." Sarov's dark eyes flashed across the nova bursting in his heads-up display, each indicating a new danger. Too many details demanded his full attention. The alien destroyer closed with them at what seemed light-speed.

"Power up on the radiation cannon," Sarov reported to the com officer. "Ready to fire. Prepare for all systems to go down."

"Mitri, please. You've got to—"

Liottey's voice vanished as Sarov initiated the program controlling the captured weapon. A loud hissing filled the control room, then the lights blinked and dropped to a twilight dimness.

"All communications circuits functioning," reported Miza. "I've got one trace on an escape capsule dropping to the surface."

"From the space station? Someone got away?" asked Sarov, still working to bring his own circuits back on-line. The radiation cannon had damaged most of his controls.

He put a half-dozen RRUs on the task of isolating and repairing. The robots would labor on until the job was completed or the ship would be unable to proceed further with partial repairs. Sarov prayed that other elements of the Death Fleet did not find them until he regained full control.

"Report on destroyer's status," he said. "I've lost all my combat sensors."

"I'm tracking five separate pieces. The cannon worked," Chikako said. "The destroyer is out of action permanently."

"So are our engines. We're drifting. The only systems still functional are yours. What about other warships in the immediate area?"

"They're ignoring us. Since our engines aren't emitting, they must think the destroyer got us even as it died—a mutual kill."

Sarov worked rapidly, then smiled. "We're drifting together with two major pieces from the destroyer."

"Agreed," Chikako said. "It appears we're near their engine section and cargo hold."

"Engine section…" mused Sarov.

"I should be in command," said Liottey. "I'm next in the chain of command. It says so in the regs."

Sarov turned, a wicked smile turning his lips into more of a sneer. "You are, Gowan, and I'm proud of you. It's damned noble of you to volunteer for such a mission. Only a selfless leader would do this."

"What? What am I doing?" the first officer asked, obviously confused. His pale-blue eyes darted around the control room, as if seeking an escape.

"You're going to jet across and enter the alien's engine room and find out why they don't blank out the way we do when they fire the radiation cannon."

"I am?"

"Mitri, he's not capable of doing anything. Look at him. He's a medical wreck. The CoolinGas burned out parts of his brain. He's even more worthless than he was before."

"Chikako," Sarov said harshly. The com officer fell silent but continued to glower at him. "Our Gowan is going across now and find what we need. Take a few ERUs with you, Gowan. We can afford to send them."

"External Retrieval Units?" Liottey said dully. "Why? What am I bringing back?"

"The switching system for their cannon," Sarov said, holding back a flare of anger. "You'll be a hero. You can prove you're worthy of commanding the *Preceptor*. No one will argue with you if you're a hero."

"Sarov, I protest."

"Log it, Chikako. I don't want to hear any more from you on this." Sarov turned back to Liottey. "Go on, prepare to jet across. We'll monitor your progress and do what we can to help…sir. We will offer only advice we can."

Gowan Liottey left, smiling foolishly. Sarov turned back to his computer and worked hard for several minutes. Repairs were proceeding too slowly for his taste. He scanned a dozen different subsections and shifted priorities to get the ship operational again in as short a time as possible. How long would they have before an alien scout ship came to investigate? They lacked the firepower to survive even a fleeting engagement.

"No Death Fleet elements interested in us," reported Chikako. "The space station is gone. I'm tracking the capsule to the planet. Do you think Tia and Norlin are in it?"

"They're survivors," Sarov said harshly. He worked furiously to balance a dozen new chores. Never had he wished for Pier Norlin more than now. Norlin lacked in-depth knowledge about any single system aboard, but he knew enough about them all to coordinate repair activities well. Sarov's specialized training had forced him to ignore so much of the cruiser's operation he felt lost, alone, beyond his ability.

He hated that feeling.

"Gowan's suited up and ready to jet across," said Chikako.

"Find the power-switching device they use to keep from blacking out their power grid when they use the radiation cannon," Sarov ordered, more to program the ERUs than for Liottey's sake.

The external CCD cameras tracked the first officer through the alien wreckage. Sarov followed the tiny spacesuited figure and the larger ERUs with the forward lasartillery battery, even though he lacked power to fire it. The threat might deter any alien countermeasure.

"I'm entering the engine compartment," radioed Liottey. "It's dark in there...Th-there are suited aliens here!"

"Your weapons, Gowan. Be careful—and use your weapons!" Sarov cried. He glanced over his shoulder at Chikako, who looked grim. He turned back to his display, feeling guilty. He shouldn't get so excited.

"You want the switch, don't you, Mitri?" the com officer asked.

"A fully functioning, multiple-firing radiation cannon would enhance the *Preceptor*'s armament," he said stiffly.

She laughed, and he hated her for it. He concentrated darkly on the vidscreen images.

"Are the aliens threatening you, Gowan?" he radioed.

"I...They're dead. I only thought they moved. The entire engine section is blasted to hell and gone. Such destruction! All the circuits are fused."

"Look for the switching device. Send the ERUs out. They know what we want. Let them roam through the hulk and trace circuits for you," urged Sarov.

"Mitri," cut in Chikako. "The main fleet has arrived. They've established orbit. I'm counting a dozen different launchers dropping mechanized fighting units. They're after the capsule."

"Thorough bastards," he muttered.

He studied his heads-up display and knew the *Preceptor* would be unable to fight—or run—for another hour, unless repair work proceeded faster than anticipated. He turned back to Gowan Liottey's hunt on the destroyer for the secret of the aliens' primary weapon.

"Heavy tanks. At least forty being transported to the surface," Chikako relayed, her voice neutral. She had turned into a conduit for information, hardly appreciating what she reported to him. Again Sarov wished Norlin was in the command chair giving orders. He found it increasingly difficult to make decisions, being completely overwhelmed with details each demanding his immediate attention. He was a tactical officer, not a commander trained in strategic analysis.

Mitri Sarov almost panicked and radioed Liottey that he could assume command. The moment of fear passed, and he came to his senses. He could never allow Liottey to command the *Preceptor*, not in such a brain-damaged condition. Giving

Liottey command even when he was at peak capacity was a major risk.

He appreciated Norlin more and more, even if he still thought of him as an interloper.

"Are any ships in the orbiting array interested in us?" he asked Miza.

"Not that I can see," she said. "They're after the escape egg and probably the mining outpost." She paused, then said, "Activity among the remainder of the fleet. They're leaving orbit. I can't tell where they're shifting, but they've left only a half-dozen of the mother ships behind."

"They know we can't do anything to them from on-planet now that the space station and the defensive net are destroyed," said Sarov, more interested in what Liottey might find than in tactical movement of the alien warships.

"Do you want me to put Gowan through directly to your display?"

"Yes," Sarov said. "He's had enough time to find the switch, if it's intact."

"...Mitri," came the first officer's anxious voice. "I don't know what to do. They're moving. I see them moving. They're dead—and they're not!"

"Quit outgassing, Gowan," Sarov said harshly. "Report."

"The ERUs have found something. Two units are on their way back with it. I don't know what it is. The aliens. They're alive, I tell you. I see them everywhere. Their monstrous bug eyes are staring at me!"

"Gowan," he said in a soothing tone. "Return to the *Preceptor*. You've done your best. Returning, you can rest in the sick bay."

"But, Mitri, they're not *dead*. They're the *enemy*. They—"

Sarov cut him off and heaved a deep sigh. "We tried. I thought he might hold up long enough to find the secret to the cannon."

Chikako's scalplock blazed a dozen different colors as inputs came at her from all quarters. She looked over her shoulder, a smile dancing on her lips.

"The ERUs just reported, Mitri. They have it. They've found the radiation cannon switch—and it's intact!"

Chapter Eight

Pier Norlin swayed, lightheaded, and sagged when his knees turned rubbery. Tia Barse supported him, her strong arm going around his waist.

"Are you all right, Cap'n?" she asked anxiously.

"The radiation burst. Its effects are finally getting to me. I don't know how much longer I can go on without medical attention." Even with her support, he slumped to the rocky floor and leaned against the smooth mine wall. Closing his eyes allowed him to drift into a different world, a more pleasant world where cool breezes blew and he ran through fields of brightly colored propeller-shaped windflowers. Ahead, he saw the dim moving shape of his Neela. He reached out to her, but she was always just beyond his fingertips. Only a tiny groan escaped his lips when he tried to call out to her.

"He's hallucinating. The radiation shorted out a portion of his brain. Look at him," came Bo Delamier's voice. Norlin tried to focus on it and failed.

"Bo, be quiet," snapped Trahnee.

The purple and vivid emerald green windflowers grew in profusion, their redolence overpowering as it filled his lungs. He inhaled deeply, then coughed. All he got was a lungful of stale air from inside his suit.

"If you two are through arguing," said Barse, "find us a way to the surface. I'm getting indications of robots coming after us again, and we're trapped in these tunnels. You killed three miners but didn't even slow the aliens' fighters. It's not much, but I want to die in the open, even if I can't see anything but methane clouds."

"A small miscalculation," Delamier said offhandedly. "You make so much out of those rock-grubbing humans."

Norlin fought through the delights surrounding him to reach out. His fingers closed on the engineer's arm. He squeezed hard enough to keep her from doing what he had tried earlier. No matter what they thought of the genhanced station commander, they had to stay together. The alien threat was too great, and as humans they couldn't bicker if they wanted to survive.

"Sorry, Cap'n," Barse said. "He thinks he's so damned superior."

"I am," Delamier said haughtily.

"You're not hallucinating?" came Trahnee's concerned voice. Norlin blinked hard and focused on her beautiful face.

"I was. Don't know why. So strange, so pretty. It was as if someone wanted me to go to sleep, to feel at peace."

"Forget that, Cap'n. The robots are closing in. What are we going to do?"

"Where are we? Did we make it into the emergency shaft?"

"It might be the shaft the miners mentioned, but there's no way we can tell since nothing is marked. There are cars on mag rails, but the tracks go off in strange directions. One even goes lower into the mines."

"Rock chewers," he said. He fought to get to his feet. The radiation had worn him down to almost nothing, destroying his cells from within. Soon, he would go into a coma and die.

"What do you mean?" asked Trahnee, staring at him as if he had turned into an alien.

"The chewers give off intense energy. They use laser drills to cut through the rock. Their ore processors radiate even more energy. They'll mask us until we can reach the surface."

"Ridiculous. Let's get into a car and head upward. We can make it. The robots won't be able to stop us," said Delamier.

"Go ahead," Norlin said. "Barse and I are going down. That's where the chewers are. They must be. Getting free of the robots is more important than reaching the surface." A strange lethargy came over him as he remembered the open fields...and Neela.

Barse helped him into a car on the magnetic track leading into the bowels of the planet. Trahnee hesitated, torn between accompanying Delamier to the surface and going with Norlin. She came to her decision. She joined Norlin and Barse.

"Oh, very well, I'll accompany you," said Delamier, sounding disgusted at such human thinking. "You'll see that I was right, and that this foolish attempt to escape will only lead to disaster."

The words had barely left his mouth when the melted-rock roof trembled, then exploded in a welter of sharp debris and cloaking dust. Norlin reached out and grabbed Delamier's arm, pulling him into the car with his fading strength. In the same motion, he fell against the single control lever and shoved it all the way forward. The magnetic car shot off at high speed and sent Norlin crashing to the floor.

"What happened?" asked Delamier, scrambling to get into a seat. He wiped the dust off his faceplate.

"The alien machines blasted their way down through the roof. They got tired of waiting for us to come to them," said Barse, venom dripping from her words.

"But that means they were above us. We...You were right!" The concept of a mere human making a correct decision had startled the genhanced officer.

Trahnee sat back and studied Norlin until he stirred uneasily on the car floor. His guts churned, and he knew the radiation was destroying his blood and intestines even as he struggled to sit up. Her scrutiny bothered him even more.

"What's wrong?" he asked her.

"You. You're different from other...humans. Are you sure you're not genhanced?"

"No!" The word came out harsher than he'd intended. He started to soften his tone, then decided against it. Trahnee might be desirable and everything a man could want—and genhanced—but too many of them were genetic freaks like Bo Delamier. The officer was egotistical and crossed the borderline between sanity and madness all too easily. What tore most at Pier Norlin was the genhanced's easy sacrifice of the three miners.

They were "only" humans.

"You chose well," Trahnee said. "The alien robots would have killed us if we had followed Bo."

"He doesn't have field experience," Norlin said. He closed his eyes, and the pain rose within him like a red tide. He tried not to drown. "I do. Sutton was a terrible way to learn what the aliens are capable of."

"Bo has experience," Trahnee said. The touch of bitterness in her voice caused Norlin to open his eyes and look at her hard.

"Where?"

"We're almost at the end of the line, Cap'n," said Barse. "The car is slowing. My sensors show the robots are close behind in the tunnel. We don't have more than five minutes before they're here."

"What are you going to do?" Trahnee asked. Her tone had changed to one of amusement, as if he had become a specimen in a giant but deadly experiment.

Norlin forced himself from the car when it stopped, and almost fell. He supported himself against the mag rail and blinked hard until his eyes focused. He almost cried when he saw the auto-med unit in an alcove. They had arrived at a nexus in the mine system where humans came to repair equipment, heal themselves, even prepare to leave and return to the surface.

As much as he wanted to go to the auto-med unit, he didn't dare. The three ponderous, laser-snouted rock chewers standing silently at the far end of the low chamber drew him. Tia Barse was already examining them. By the time he reached her side, she had completed her survey.

"They aren't tanks, Cap'n, but they might do."

"You intend to use them against combat robots?" scoffed Delamier. Norlin ignored him.

Circling the nearest rock chewer, Norlin estimated its lifetime against an alien robot tank. Not long, he decided, but it would be good enough. He slipped into the narrow niche behind the control panel and braced himself as he programmed the chewer's limited computer. The machine lumbered forward, a corona discharge starting to form around its blunted prow as it sought something to lase.

He hopped out, stumbled and fell. The rock chewer's laser drill clicked on and began firing on the robots appearing at the end of the shaft. He had circumvented enough of the chewer's programming to cause it to "see" the robots as solid rock wall. The restricted movement of the chewer, however, caused it to quickly fall prey to the more mobile combat robots.

Their vicious cross-fire destroyed it within ten seconds.

Tia Barse launched a second chewer. Five more of the alien robots died, two from the laser drill and three under its ponderous treads as it /crawled forward to chew through a nonexistent wall. It, too, turned to slag under withering fire.

An explosion brought down the ceiling at the far end of the chamber, momentarily blocking the attacking robots' line of fire. By the time they had tunneled through and once more sought their human prey, the third and final rock chewer's laser drill lashed out. The robots vaporized.

Norlin looked up. Trahnee had sent the third chewer on its course of destruction—and it had saved them.

"Thank you," he said.

The world turned milky as his corneas fogged from the radiation he had suffered what seemed a lifetime ago. He sank down, then fell face forward.

* * *

Seconds later, Pier Norlin snapped to consciousness. He jerked around, banged his head and tried to run. The nightmares faded, and only soft, gentle dreams entered his head. They, too, drifted away, and he realized he sat in the dusty mine nexus, laser-drilled tunnels running off in all directions.

The auto-med unit stood beside him, humming contentedly, small green indicator lights burning steadily. Several probes ran through his emergency spacesuit and into his arms and legs.

He checked the readout on the unit and saw that the worst of the radiation effects had been adequately countered—for the moment. The heavy ionizing radiation burst he had taken required more than a simple portable mine automed to repair, but the most immediate symptoms were gone. Longer-range chromosome and genetic damage needed more subtle repairing. Those could wait, though.

He was alive and had defeated the alien killers sent after them.

For the moment.

"Tia," he called. He had to adjust the volume level of his radio. The feedback almost deafened him. "Tia, report!"

"Don't get your blood pressure up, Cap'n," she said. "I've got a dozen of the robots spotted, but they're working systematically through the upper levels. I can't say for sure, but it looks as if they ran into another crew of miners."

"Can we warn them?"

Barse shook her head. He saw her colorless eyes through the spacesuit visor turn desolate. "We don't dare. We'll draw the robots like falling into a black hole if we do."

"You should have obeyed my orders," Delamier said. He strutted over and glared at Norlin. "We are trapped here with no way out. The aliens will pick off the small bands of miners until only we remain. They will make short shrift of us when they detect our all too obvious heat signatures."

"No thanks to you," Norlin said. "You haven't done much to help since we landed on Renfro." He pushed himself to his feet and found strength returning and his vision clearing. Tiny black spots told him that his eyes may have been burned in several places and his hands shook uncontrollably, but he was alive and for that he had to give thanks.

Trahnee stood to one side. He went toward her, stopping only when he reached the end of the probes from the automedic that held him on a leash.

"I appreciate what you did," he said simply.

"For what?" One eyebrow lifted in surprise. He couldn't see much more of her face because of the bright overhead light shining off her spacesuit visor.

"You started the third rock chewer just when we needed it."

"I want to live, too," she said, shrugging. "You are the best chance we have for escape from this rock box."

Delamier glared at her, then spun and stalked off.

Not for the first time, Norlin wondered at the pair's relationship. They acted more like lovers having a fight than brother and sister.

"We have to contact the *Preceptor*," he said. He swallowed hard as the thought came to him that his cruiser might have been destroyed along with the space station. The Death Fleet left little to chance once it began its attack. If it was human or human-built and moved, it received total attention until annihilated.

"Getting a signal through the rock is a problem, Cap'n. I wish Chikako was here. She would know how to do it." Barse then chuckled. "If she was here we wouldn't have to radio her. We could just shout at her."

"A signal?" Trahnee repeated. "There might be a way." She paused. "Do you want to save the miners—or us?"

"Both," he answered. Then he understood what she meant. Would he sacrifice their lives to insure the miners' continued existence?

He shook his head to indicate that he would not. The Empire Service defended the colonists along the frontier, but his mission took on greater importance than any single world. By now the alien fleet had shifted for another system, possibly a more populated one. A few thousand miners' deaths meant nothing compared to saving a larger colony of tens of millions.

"The robots will believe the miners are responsible. The tragedy is that the miners might never even detect the signal."

"Can the *Preceptor* pick up the signal?" demanded Barse.

"If your communications officer is alert, yes," answered Trahnee.

"Try," was all Norlin could say.

He sat impatiently and let the auto-med continue its work on him while Trahnee pirated what remained of the rock chewers, the alien robots and a dozen supply boxes in the stope to put together an odd-looking device.

"I'm going to use the magnetic rails for antennae. The coded bursts are broadcast—they'll cover a wide frequency spectrum. Your com officer—"

"Chikako Miza," Norlin said, the officer's name somehow important to him. If he mouthed it often enough, Chikako would not only hear the message but respond. It was crazy, but it gave him hope.

"Chikako will decipher the simple coded bursts." Trahnee flipped a toggle. "The alignment computer from the rock chewer will control the broadcast."

"What about a reply?"

"The computer will record it, if it comes."

"*When* it comes," Norlin corrected.

"Of course," the genhanced woman said, obviously humoring him. "When it comes."

Chikako Miza's reply came four hours later.

Chapter Nine

"It'll act as a diversion," Pier Norlin said, not really believing it for an instant. "The miners will be able to get free of the aliens' attack if we create a big enough distraction."

Bo Delamier sniffed at such an absurd notion. Trahnee said nothing, but Norlin read the genhanced woman's feelings well. She didn't believe it, either. He wasn't so sure he bought into the idea, but they had nothing else to try.

"Do you think Sarov has the radiation cannon sighted in properly?" Tia Barse asked nervously. "We don't even know what the damned thing does. It just does it well."

"We can only hope he hooked in the switching device properly. I don't want the *Preceptor* to draw attention to itself and then go dead in space."

The brief communication between ship and down-planet party had been brief but heartfelt. Just knowing the others were alive bolstered their spirits and gave a modicum of hope they might get out of this with their skins intact.

Norlin kept thinking of the planet beamers still orbiting Renfro II. Any one of them was more than a match for the

Preceptor, even with its full combat capacity. If Sarov fired the radiation cannon and blew the ship's power supply again, switch or no switch, they were all dead.

"They'll find us," Delamier said confidently. "I know we didn't eliminate all the robot hunters because I felt unexplained vibrations through the rock. I am very sensitive to such things."

He peered into the depths of the mine, as if he could see them coming. Norlin ignored him. Delamier might have augmented physical senses, too, for all he knew, but none of that mattered unless he shared what he knew in a timely fashion. All Norlin could tell was that the genhanced officer liked to gloat rather than forewarn.

The rock chewers had stopped the alien machines for a short while—it had to be long enough for the *Preceptor* to act. Still, he worried—it had been almost six hours since they had destroyed the robots and one since Chikako Miza had told them about the *Preceptor*'s foray.

"Got it," cried Barse. "The beam's coming in. Take cover, if you want."

"Why bother?" Norlin asked. The destructive lance of pure energy from the captured radiation cannon couldn't be stopped by any shielding he had seen. Cowering behind a pile of crushed gravel hardly seemed adequate protection against a weapon capable of laying en entire world to waste.

The explosion lifted him from his feet and sent him skidding along the rocky floor. He felt the outer laminated layer of the spacesuit ripping away. The inner held, and he didn't lose any of his precious air to the poisonous gases filling the mine shaft.

"Look at that," marveled Barse. She stared straight up.

The *Preceptor*'s beam had slashed directly through two kilometers of rock and vaporized a channel through the methane and ammonia atmosphere, making it seem as if they could climb directly to the stars winking hard and bright at the top. The column blazed by the radiation cannon beam vanished quickly in the turbulence, and the normal atmosphere poured back into the artificially cut strait.

"Do we climb out?" asked Delamier. "That's a long way to go."

"Radio the miners," Norlin ordered his engineer. "Tell them what's happening."

"Heavy interference, Cap'n. The aliens are blocking the usual channels."

"I'll try. I am very good at such things," said Trahnee.

Norlin nodded. He had other things to worry about. How long would it take Sarov to drop a shuttle down to the surface and lower a line for them to get out? The back of his neck itched. He knew the robot killers stirred throughout the mine and sought them. He closed his eyes and took a shallow breath of the stale air in his pressure suit, knowing the aliens weren't after him personally. They simply eradicated all organic life wherever they found it, and if he happened to be in the way, he was a dead man.

Along with the others. Along with Trahnee. This thought filled him with a surge of irrational fear. Her life mattered more than all the others combined. Let the miners get crushed under the alien assault crafts' tracks. Let his crew perish in the wink of a radiation blast. And Delamier meant nothing, if only Trahnee was saved.

"There's the shuttle flare," said Barse. "It'll be just a few minutes now."

"We won't make it," said Delamier. "This is a vacuum-brained scheme."

"Stay here if you don't want to try it," snapped Norlin. He was apprehensive enough about their escape and getting Trahnee to safety. He didn't need the genhanced officer telling him how dangerous it was, because they all knew the odds were against them.

"I got through. The miners have scattered," reported Trahnee. "I don't think we will be able to save many—or any."

Norlin balled his fists then forced himself to relax. His mission in the Renfro II system had been a complete failure. The Death Fleet had sailed in and done its work before shifting away. The mobile killers they had left behind were enough to take care of the unorganized miners. He tensed again thinking of how Bo Delamier had failed so completely in his duty as station commander. He had been warned. He could have done more.

Elaborate defensive systems and holograms weren't enough against the aliens and their methodical, genocidal warfare.

"Here's the line—a basket is attached. Everyone in," called Barse.

Norlin followed Trahnee and his engineer into the metal cage. He didn't wait to see if Delamier would join them.

"Up!" he ordered.

At the last possible instant, the genhanced space station commander jumped and caught the edge so Trahnee could pull him in. She turned her grey, penetrating eyes on Norlin and stared.

He wasn't uncomfortable under the lovely woman's scrutiny. He simply wondered what raced through her mind. He had no idea what she thought, what she felt, what motivated her—and it surprised him that he wanted to know. If he could find out, he could do more to please her.

The metal basket banged from side to side as the monomolecular line quickly reeled them to the surface. The instant they emerged into the swirling winds of methane and ammonia, the aliens struck. Energy weapons crackled and ionized the gases around them, creating miniature lightning storms that sent bolts of sizzling electricity into the grounded cage. Barse yelled something about a missile; Norlin couldn't tell what she said because he'd grabbed Trahnee and dived, taking them both away from the metal cage.

The alien robots homed in on the dense metal like bees looking for pollen. The basket blew apart seconds after Norlin jumped free with the genhanced woman. He scrambled to his feet and took stock of the situation.

"Who's inside?" he asked. The shuttle had landed a dozen meters away and sealed up tight after sending out the robot to lower the cage to them.

"Lt. Liottey, sir."

Norlin groaned. Why had Sarov sent the first officer on this mission? He realized it had to be for one reason only—in his condition, Liottey was expendable.

"Lay down a covering barrage. Light countermeasures missiles, whatever lasartillery capacity you have—use them all. Get us out of here!"

A few feeble winks from a low-power continuous-wave laser flashed through the atmosphere, ionizing the gases to dancing motes all around in response to his order. Norlin cursed. The shuttle carried minimal armament, most of it designed for light retrenchment and earth-moving. It had never been intended for fighting a full-scale battle.

"Get in. Hurry!"

Barse and Trahnee slid in as the shuttle bay door opened. Delamier was slower to follow. Norlin wished he could simply leave the genhanced officer behind. Instead of acting on this impulse, he waited for him to climb aboard then dived after, hit the bay door switch and radioed Liottey, "Get us out of here. Hurry!"

"But, sir, several regulations concerning take-offs require you to be safely buckled into a—"

"Now!" Norlin roared. "Get us out of here now!"

Liottey mumbled about important regulations but obeyed. The abrupt acceleration slammed Norlin into the far wall of the cargo bay. He clung on to a stanchion until his arms turned to lead. The blast continued; he weakened further under the intense acceleration. He heard the roar of atmosphere past the shuttle's hull diminish, and still he held on. He thought he felt vibrations caused by nearby missile explosions but wasn't sure. That would have had to be transmitted by the atmosphere, but they were in space now. They had to be.

He was still clinging to the stanchion when Tia Barse came back and shook him.

"It's all right, Cap'n. We've docked with the *Preceptor*. We're home."

He stared at her numbly. He ached all over and, more than anything else, his arms hurt. He managed to ask, "Status? What about the Death Fleet?"

"We're picking up elements in orbit. Sarov thinks one may be coming after us—a big one."

"Let's get the hell out of here. We can't do anything for the poor devils below." He closed his eyes and shuddered. He had been sent to warn the miners and others like them of the menace posed by the aliens, and he had failed. The aliens had raped another human-settled world and had done so virtually untouched. Only the handful destroyed by Bo Delamier's defense net had paid any price at all for attacking a human-colonized world.

"We got it," Barse said. "I haven't had time to do more than glance at it, but we have it."

"What do we have?" His mind refused to believe he no longer had to clutch the hull support. Norlin wobbled a bit as he walked but refused his engineer's help.

"Their switch. Chikako told you Liottey retrieved it from a derelict. We can use the radiation cannon now and not cripple ourselves. We can, that is, after it's hooked up properly. Sarov is a complete loss at such things—he says he didn't have time to tend to it. Just be happy it worked well enough to keep the ship from becoming a derelict when he fired to get us off-planet. It didn't exhaust our energy too much; it just blew a few unimportant circuits."

Norlin should have rejoiced, but he was drained of all emotion and wanted only to sleep. Nodding, he pushed past her, picked up the ship's cat and tried to pet it, only to be rebuffed. Neutron didn't like the feel of spacesuit material against his fur and let the captain know it with a quick swipe of his claws.

Norlin tossed the cat down and began stripping off his suit. He had work to do.

He had to get them out of the system alive.

"Pier," came Trahnee's seductive voice. He stared at her, the lethargy vanishing. "Where are we going?"

"After the Death Fleet. We have to try to stop them. That's our mission."

"I want to go to Porlock V."

"Why there?" Norlin shook his head, trying to clear it. His frontier upbringing had been far more puritanical than he might have received on Earth or another inner world closer to Emperor Arian's court. Porlock was a pleasure world; although its people ought to be warned of the threat facing them, Norlin knew of a dozen others with manufacturing, research and educational institutions more deserving of his time and effort. If all couldn't be saved or adequately warned, the most important ought to head the priority list.

Porlock V was far from being important to mankind's survival.

"We're following the Death Fleet," he said. "I'm certain Chikako got a bearing on them when they shifted."

"Porlock," Trahnee said in a soft, soothing voice. "We should go to Porlock. It is important to me, Pier. Porlock V."

"No." Even as he spoke, he felt his resolve weakening. There were reasons to follow the aliens, yet saving the frontier colonies was an important mission. If the *Preceptor* went to Porlock V, the word could be spread more quickly. Many ships visited the pleasure planet. They could carry the message back to their home worlds, giving even more the chance to prepare and defend themselves.

"Please, Pier," Trahnee said. Her grey eyes seemed to grow and turn into pools sucking him into an endless vortex. "I want you to do this for me. We can't defeat the aliens without help. Porlock can provide it."

Norlin started to argue. Porlock had no defensive capability—or none that he remembered. Better to warn those who could aid themselves. Yet he couldn't deny the logic of spreading his warning rapidly through the heavy space traffic enjoyed by the planet.

He cycled through the double hull and armor ports and entered the control room. Chikako Miza's shaved head gleamed pink, the tall, dark scalplock glowing reassuringly with the sensors woven through it. Stolid Mitri Sarov glanced in his direction then turned back to the battle simulation he studied so intently on his vidscreen. Tactics were more important than niceties such as acknowledging the presence of his commanding officer.

It felt good to be back, Norlin decided. He dropped into his command chair and rapidly checked the *Preceptor*'s condition. Only Gowan Liottey had been negligent in his work, and this came as no real surprise considering the officer's mental condition. Norlin punched up the first officer's medical report and entered a notation to relieve Liottey of all duties and put him full-time on the auto-med for rehabilitation. Too many portions of his brain had been damaged by the CoolinGas to trust him with any detail, no matter how trivial or how much the ship needed every able-bodied officer at their station.

"Porlock medical facilities can restore his behavior patterns," Trahnee said from behind. Norlin jumped. He hadn't realized she had followed him into the control room. "They pride themselves on their knowledge of brain function and chemistry."

"That's because they develop psycho-active drugs for recreation," he said.

"Yes, and more. Research. They can help."

Norlin's fingers twitched as he started to enter the commands into the navigational computer that would blast them away from the Renfro system. Where did he want to go? After the Death Fleet or to Porlock?

He decided.

Chikako's sensors blinked red, as if they had a life of their own and had turned angry at his decision. Sarov glowered at him. The feathery scars under the man's left eye pulsed pinkly, but he was not driven to comment. Only Tia Barse complained, and he cut her off with a savage gesture. She was only the engineer. He was the captain. He made the decisions.

He had decided to go to Porlock V.

Chapter Ten

"We can die of old age waiting for them to do their jobs," grumbled Tia Barse.

Norlin sat in his command chair and fumed. He switched constantly from one heads-up display to another, barely seeing the flashing readouts and the messages they sent. He did it only to distract himself from the pissed-off engineer—and the feeling that she was right.

They should never have come to Porlock V.

"Let Bo try again," urged Trahnee. "He has a way with petty bureaucrats like this one."

"He tried already," Norlin said, disgusted. "His best efforts got us another fourteen hours in the clearance queue. They aren't that busy."

"I can lay a small barrage of timed-detonation missiles across their space station's orbit, Captain," offered Sarov. "That might wake them up. There wouldn't be hardly any orbital debris left, if I did it right."

"I've worked out their com-link codes," cut in Chikako Miza. Her sensors winked on and off slowly, little traffic going through her board. "Scrambling it would be easy. Those shuttles going down to the planet would never arrive without proper guidance. Their pilots are..."

"No," Norlin said. He swung about in the chair and faced Trahnee. He seethed at the delay and at himself. She had convinced him this was the way to spread the word about the threat posed by the alien fleet. Why had he allowed himself to be so easily swayed?

He started to order her from the control room, then paused. She had a way about her that appealed mightily to him. He no longer denied that. He might even love her, even if she was genhanced and, to her, he was a "mere" human. He swallowed hard. From the way she looked at him, the feelings of love might be mutual. Her grey eyes burned with passion, and a flush came to brighten her pale cheeks.

He stabbed his finger down on the relay button that connected him with Porlock's Port Authority. He leaned back, waited for a response, then said, "This is Empire Service Cruiser *Preceptor*. We have a small emergency on board."

"What's that, *Preceptor*?" came the indolent reply. "Not enough liquor in your tanks? We can send over a tug-full of whatever you want. The handlers are trained to—"

"One missile is aimed directly at the center of your station. I can't tell if it will fire or not."

"Is this a threat?"

"A warning," corrected Norlin, beginning to enjoy the exchange. "You have my full report on the Death Fleet. You know we suffered some minor circuit damage. This missile might home in and blow you into micron-sized dust."

"Depart immediately. Clearance unauthorized for..."

"That's not going to help you. This is a deep space missile. The only way you can be sure it won't hit you is if we're safely docked. That way, the firing tube will always be aimed away from the station."

Norlin shifted his attention from the defensive systems display and looked at Trahnee. She smiled broadly. He basked in her approval. He quickly checked the sensors again to be sure the Port Authority didn't attempt to open fire on them to remove this supposed menace.

He need not have worried. Their defensive capability was pitiful. The lasartillery batteries intended to protect the station had been dismantled and colorful laser beacons installed. Instead of deadly lances of pure energy, he saw vivid images advertising a half-dozen different pleasure jaunts on the planet below. They had taken spacial advertising to an entirely new level, and one he was not inclined to think highly of.

He had found only small launch tubes, which *might* send forth a cloud of gnat-sized missiles designed to pepper a ship's hull and create thousands of small holes. The way the Port Authority operated, Norlin wasn't sure they had any defensive systems left.

The alien fleet would find Porlock an easy victory, but then, it did with most human worlds.

"Permission to dock granted," came back the agitated voice. He hesitated, wanting to force the Port Authority controller to show his face. Standard procedure called for vidscreen contact. Porlock's space station had avoided it, as if the *Preceptor* were a contaminated vessel and the slightest contact, even visual, might be infectious.

"Thank you," Norlin said in satisfaction. He touched the appropriate toggles to begin the docking maneuver. "All systems stand down," he ordered. He heaved a sigh of relief when he felt the small bump that signaled successful docking.

They were finally on the Porlock space station. Now he needed to find the station commander and talk with him.

"Cap'n, do we have to stay aboard?" asked Barse. "I'm sick of looking at these walls…"

"And you've heard about the fleshpots offered down on Porlock," he finished for her. He hesitated to authorized leave for his crew. Yet they deserved it, and Porlock was a perfect port.

"The *Preceptor* will be safe if you leave it under seal," Trahnee said. "They should have some time to themselves. We have been in space such a long time."

Norlin didn't bother telling her that they had been aboard the *Preceptor* longer than she imagined. Since leaving Sutton II, they had enjoyed little recreational time, even with the few diversions provided aboard the ship. The constant struggle against the Death Fleet hadn't allowed that. Even before going against the aliens, just after he had assumed command, there had been no chance to rest.

"Shore leave for those who want it," he said, hoping Sarov might prefer to stay aboard and reenact his war games on the tactical computer. Somewhat to his surprise, Sarov was the first to shut down his board and prepare to leave. Chikako Miza followed his lead, and Barse had started powering down the instant Trahnee had spoken.

This worried Norlin. *He* had made the decision to allow leave for the crew, not the genhanced woman. Did his engineer think Trahnee had such power over him that he gave in to her every whim? It wasn't that way. It wasn't.

"What about Liottey?" asked Chikako. "Should we lock him up?"

"Take him with us," urged Trahnee. "The doctors on-planet might be able to restore him fully. They are experts in dealing with brain chemical imbalances."

Norlin snorted at this—they tailored recreational drugs for individual body chemistries. Still, it might work in Gowan Liottey's favor rather than against him. If nothing else, the doctors might fabricate tranquilizers to keep him stable and quiet.

"All down to the planet," he said, with some misgivings about leaving the ship without any crew.

He finished a probe of the space station—it had been stripped of all important electronics. Only a decorated shell orbited the planet.

* * *

They trooped through the deserted station interior and went to the main office. A frightened controller sat in a glasteel booth, door locked securely against the madmen from the Empire Service cruiser.

"The missile isn't going to damage the station, is it?" the man asked immediately.

"It's pointed into space. I wouldn't want to go aboard my vessel to check it, though," Norlin said. "Other circuits are at the point of malfunction. We're especially worried about the radiation block circuit governor in the engine compartment. It might flood the entire space station with hard radiation if the…well, you don't want to hear about uninteresting details like that, do you? If no one boards my ship, nothing untoward will happen." He barely kept from smiling at this veiled threat when he saw how effective it was with the Port Authority controller.

"You have to use your own shuttle to go down," the controller said. "None of our regular staff wants to pilot you. We don't like the idea of adding to the ESers on-planet."

"Agreed," Norlin said, wondering what the man meant. He heaved a sigh of relief, though. He didn't want to be at the mercy of some drugged planetary taxi driver. "I would like to see the transmission log between the *Preceptor* and your office," he said, seeing that his crew, Trahnee and Delamier had gone to a docking bay to wait for him to retrieve their shuttle.

"On the screen," the controller said.

As the transcription flashed past on the vidscreen, Norlin's temper flared. He had allowed Bo Delamier to contact the Porlock space station because Trahnee had said the genhanced officer could get them a quick docking. Delamier had done everything he could to deny them entry and make it seem as if the Port Authority objected to having any ship commanded by Pier Norlin in dock.

"Jealous," muttered Norlin under his breath. He had seen the way Delamier glared at him when Trahnee was with him.

He never had figured out the relationship between the two genhanced. At times it was platonic, at others they might be mistaken for lovers. Still other times, they acted like brother and sister.

Even worse, he couldn't describe his own feelings toward Trahnee—or hers for him.

He shook it off and hurried back to the *Preceptor*. A quick check of the safety systems assured him his ship would remain in dock undisturbed. He took a spare com-link and adjusted it to the ship's primary control frequency; he could monitor most systems from on-planet and, if necessary, initiate limited action.

The short flight to the planet proved tense for him. His crew was anxious to be on their own, and Delamier sat quietly, a peculiar smile curling his lips, as if he knew something no one else did. Trahnee's composure kept Norlin from worrying unduly about the genhanced officer's secret, whatever it might be. Their goals might be different, but their paths coincided for the moment. Delamier wasn't likely to do anything to damage either the shuttle or the *Preceptor*.

Norlin powered down the shuttle and opened the airlock to fresh air that flowed like a fine vintage wine into the cramped, stuffy vessel.

"Enjoy yourselves," he told Barse, Sarov and Miza. "Stay in touch, though." He tapped the com-link fastened to his belt. The crew carried similar units.

"Don't worry about us, Cap'n," said Barse. "We know how to orbit clear of trouble." She paused as her colorless eyes fixed on Liottey. "Is he going to be all right? I never liked the son of a bitch, but I like him even less in this condition."

"We will see to it," Trahnee said reassuringly. Barse scowled at the genhanced woman then left without another word.

"I need to find the planetary governor," Norlin said. "I might be able to convince him of the trouble ahead, even if the Port Authority controller wasn't persuaded."

"You worry so, Pier," said Trahnee. "The Death Fleet's arrival isn't imminent. Let's take care of poor Gowan and then enjoy ourselves. You and I and Bo can find such fine pleasures."

"Liottey first," he agreed. He felt uneasy at the prospect of the two genhanced and him finding any "fine pleasures." Their imperial, sophisticated tastes might prove too much for him and his simpler standards.

They left the shuttle in the middle of the landing field and hopped onto a small computer-controlled vehicle going toward a cluster of buildings at the edge of the tarmac.

"The field looks deserted. I thought there would be much more activity than there is. From everything I'd heard, Porlock was a busy port."

The words had barely left his lips when he smelled ozone. Norlin jerked around, instantly alert. The soft wind blowing across the field came from the buildings. He strained hard and heard a soft buzzing sound peculiar to combat laserifles.

His hand flashed to his sidearm. Trahnee restrained him.

"No," she said in her soft, seductive voice. "Do not worry. There is no trouble."

"Someone's firing a laserifle," he said, "and we're going straight toward them." He tried to divert the small vehicle and failed. He started to use his pistol on the controls, but Bo Delamier stopped him.

"You'll make it worse if you show your weapon," the genhanced officer said. His blue eyes had turned to chips of diamond, hard, cold and shining with excitement. He settled back down but remained alert. "Let's ride it out. We're in no danger."

Norlin sat back, tensed and ready for a fight. This was a pleasure planet, not a combat zone—or so he'd thought.

Their vehicle came to a silent halt outside the building he suspected of being the source of the ozone.

"Welcome to Porlock V," came a booming computer-generated voice. "How may we serve you? Accommodations? Viands from all of known space? More diverting…recreations?"

"Information," Norlin said before the others could speak. "Status on the battle in progress."

"The rebels are once more defeated," the voice replied. "Emperor Arian rejoices anew at our devoted servants who die for his exalted honor!"

"Casualty report," Norlin requested. Trahnee tried to quiet him. He shot her a cold, hard look that made her back away.

"Four rebels dead, two injured. Two Civil Regulators slightly wounded. Peace is restored in our planetary paradise. Visitors need not worry for their personal safety…unless you specifically request an intense diversion."

"How long has the civil war been going on?" Norlin asked. Civil disorder flared on many planets along the frontier. The farther from Earth and Emperor Arian's court, the more likely a planet's population was to protest the heavy taxes and lack of attention from the Inner Worlds. In part, this paucity of protection fostered the Death Fleet's easy victory over planet after colony planet.

"We now enter the fifteen month of unrest. I reiterate that it is of no concern to you as a visitor."

"Agreed," Norlin said. He saw Trahnee relax as he spoke. Bo Delamier stood behind him, out of his line of sight. "We need a doctor for our friend." Gowan Liottey had sat in the vehicle motionless and silent the entire while.

"I am equipped to perform modest medical examinations. If you remain in this vehicle, it will take you to a specialist I have determined to be perfect for the malady."

"Your diagnosis?" asked Norlin, suspicious of a greeting robot's ability.

"Inhalation of CoolinGas and subsequent brain deterioration caused by chemical imbalance. Am I accurate?"

"You are," he admitted, still not trusting such remote computer-driven analysis.

"Let the vehicle take Gowan to the doctor. We can seek other paths," urged Trahnee.

Norlin knew there wouldn't be any problem. The few worlds he had seen with elaborate computer-controlled environments such as this one functioned well and prevented humans from damaging themselves too badly. He gave specific orders to the welcoming computer concerning Liottey. As the small vehicle drove off with his first officer in it, However, he felt a pang of regret. It was as if he had abandoned his crew—or they had finally abandoned him.

"He'll be fine, Pier. They know how to take care of visitors. Believe me," Trahnee said. And he did.

She took his arm and walked close to his side, and he believed—for the moment—that everything might work out for them.

"Let's find somewhere nice to stay, then we can arrange to meet with the planetary governor."

"You two go on," said Delamier. "I'll find the governor."

"No!" snapped Norlin. He subsided. He didn't want to confront Delamier yet about tying them up in red tape on arrival. The log had also shown considerable com activity to the planet. Who had Delamier contacted—and why?

"It's all right, Pier. Trust me," soothed Trahnee.

"Go on," Norlin said. He didn't trust Delamier—and he wasn't sure he trusted Trahnee, either. That caused a pang of regret. He wanted to. He found her enticingly beautiful and more exciting than any woman he had ever met, including Neela Cosarrian, now long dead.

"Good. Come along, Pier. Let me show you a few of the tamer recreations. We have time. We do," Trahnee assured him.

In spite of his misgivings, Norlin found himself relaxing—and falling even more in love with the genhanced woman.

Chapter Eleven

"I've never experienced anything like this," Pier Norlin said. Trahnee took his arm and guided him from the Sensory Palace, an unimposing rock melt building he wouldn't have given a second look at an hour earlier. Inside the simple structure, however, he had found hopes and dreams fulfilled, and now, all too soon they exited to the street, dazed.

"No drugs, Pier. I promised. You did enjoy it, didn't you?" she asked anxiously.

"I did," he said, still in awe of the experience. He had drifted and floated in an electronic haze of direct cortical stimulation. Whims became reality. Reality became…even more. The past sailed through his mind, a familiar ghost. The future became a fresh, brisk wind lifting him from his gloomy mood. And the present became so intense he'd wanted to cry.

Trahnee had.

He reached over and brushed the last of her tears from her cheeks. On impulse, he kissed her lightly. The simple, fleeting touch proved more electric and vital than anything he had experienced within the Sensory Palace. She was more than hopes and ambitions realized. She was love incarnate.

"I love you, Pier," she said in a low voice. More tears poured down her cheeks. "I don't know how it happened, but I do."

"Because I'm not genhanced, it shouldn't happen?" he asked, a touch of bitterness finding its way into his voice. He wasn't sure if he was more offended by the implication or his own feelings toward her.

"Bo and I..." she began, searching for the proper words and not finding them. "Bo and I have been together for so long."

"Just together?" he asked, still unsure of their relationship. What she said turned it into something more than sibling love, but what she meant confused him.

"He's ambitious. I need that in a man. Bo is capable, too." She heaved a deep, shuddering breath and fought to get her emotions under control. "You're ambitious and capable, too, my darling Pier, but you're not genhanced. You can't know what that means in Emperor Arian's court."

"If someone hasn't tinkered with my genes, I can't get very far?"

"That's it. The emperor doesn't state it as bluntly, but that is his policy. Ordinary humans have done so poorly throughout Earth history that the hope of the race rests with the genetically enhanced alone. It is a terrible burden we bear, but we are capable of success against any odds."

"The hope of the race depends on defeating the Death Fleet," Norlin said.

"Genhanced officers can do it."

"Bo didn't, I did. I have done so repeatedly. We have to be careful, but we can meet them one-on-one and win."

"I know." Trahnee sucked in a lungful of the fresh, clean, invigorating air and stared ahead. Norlin started to speak when he caught another whiff of ozone from a laserifle. Without breaking stride, he took her arm and steered her down an immaculately swept alley. Even the trash in the bins seemed to be sanitized before being discarded.

"What's wrong?" she asked.

"Laser fire. I can smell it." He drew his sidearm and checked its charge. The laser pistol lacked the cyclic impact of a combat laserifle but carried enough force to slow an armored attacker. He wished he had brought his explosive pellet pistol. That weapon could match an ancient howitzer for firepower.

The skirmish erupting in the street confirmed his worst suspicions. He pushed Trahnee down behind a discarded crate and aimed his pistol toward the mouth of the alley, ready for any intrusion. The fight went on in plain sight in the street, but no one darted in his direction or even noticed him.

"Rebels fighting the Empire Service troops," he said softly. He lifted his pistol to fire.

Trahnee stopped him.

"Don't. Let them fight it out. This isn't your battle."

"It is," he said. "I'm an officer in the Empire Service. I'm sworn to uphold the law, even if it means killing civilians." His face hardened. "Especially if it means killing rebels." He had little sympathy for those attempting to overthrow the government forcibly, although on some worlds it had proven to be the only way to bring desperately needed change. He had argued with Neela Cosarrian about this; she had warned him his stand for the emperor, right or wrong, would bring him disaster.

The more he saw of Emperor Arian and his minions, the more he thought his lover had been right. Still, he had sworn to uphold the civil peace. He risked his own life and that of his crew to defend the star frontier from the Death Fleet. Internal unrest on this planet meant poor defense against the marauding aliens.

"I can't let—" He stopped in mid-sentence when he saw Bo Delamier on the far side of the street with a com-link in his hand. He keyed his own com-unit, then felt a cold lump form in his belly. They both used the same frequency. Delamier was analyzing the ES soldiers' position then relaying information to the rebels, giving them much-needed intel to avoid the soldiers' counterattacks. Norlin listened for several seconds, hoping he was wrong and that the genhanced officer wasn't betraying? the Empire Service troops struggling and dying in the rebel ambush.

When the rebels moved apart and withering fire from farther down the street cut the soldiers to bloody ribbons, Norlin knew his suspicion was right. Bo Delamier aided the insurgents.

"I'm sorry, Pier. It has to be this way," Trahnee said.

"What's going on? He's helping the rebels ambush the emperor's troops. You're both from Earth. You support Emperor Arian."

"It might be difficult for you to understand," she said, "but there is little hope for significant advancement in Arian's court. Even we genhanced find it almost impossible, if we aren't directly related to the emperor."

"You and Bo have been attempting to overthrow one colonial government after another," Norlin realized, the small pieces fitting together to give him a larger, more desolate view of the woman he thought he loved and her companion.

"Why do you think someone of Bo's ability was placed in command of the Renfro space station? The planet and its mines are important, but the assignment was far beneath his social position or his mental ability."

"You were exiled there when other attempted coups failed."

"Yes," she said without any show of guilt. "Bo is capable but unstable. He had victory within his grasp twice before and let it slip away because of impatience. His ambition soared when he should have consolidated his gains. He can be so hard to convince at times." She sighed. "Perhaps Porlock will be different. We heard about this revolt several months ago and knew it was perfect for what we must do. It's much better organized than on Windsor or Arbogast."

"That's why you wanted to come here instead of going after the Death Fleet."

"We know the worlds where the governments have slipped and the tide rises against them. This is the one where we can most likely succeed. Bo will be ruler of this planet within a month. His analysis proves it. When he is control, we can spread the word about the aliens. So, you see, Pier, you did right bringing us here. You will save countless lives because the ruler of an entire planet like Porlock commands so much more attention than the captain of a space cruiser."

"Why not quash the rebellion and gain the emperor's gratitude? He'd put Bo in charge of the world and—"

"Poor Pier," she said pityingly. "Living on the edge of civilization has given you an exaggerated notion of risk and reward. Out here, if you take a risk you can reap commensurate bounty for it. It doesn't work that way in Emperor Arian's court. We might put down this revolt and find an imperial cousin in command, one who had curried favor most recently or performed well in some other way."

"That's probably what caused this rebellion," Norlin said. "You have to recognize talent and promote those best able to command."

"You do have a grasp of the situation," she said earnestly. "Help us. You and Bo can crush the local garrison. They deal with rowdy drunks and those too intoxicated on drugs to function well. They aren't soldiers, not like the two of you. We can win if you help!"

Norlin fought the tug of her softly passionate, suasive words.

"Is that all you want? To rule a world?" He shook his head. "You could do it. Delamier is able enough, but why do you have to accomplish it by insurrection? Men and women are dying out there." He shuddered as he realized that people dying meant nothing to Trahnee. They weren't genhanced. They were only humans.

"Porlock isn't important to you, Pier. You had to be cajoled to even come here. Let Bo help the rebels."

"Let Bo destroy this world from the inside out, you mean." His pistol came up, and he fired at the genhanced officer. The flickering beam of coherent light burned through the wall to one side of Delamier's head. Norlin's target moved a fraction of a centimeter, hardly noticing the brush with death.

Norlin moved to the far side of the alley to get a better shot. When Delamier died, the skirmish in the street would die, too. He guided it expertly; without the head, the body of the rebellion would thrash around for a while and then die. He at least knew now what the genhanced officer had done during the delay in docking—and whom he had contacted on-planet.

He missed again when the surge of battle clogged the mouth of the alley. For the first time, a rebel noticed him. Norlin didn't recognize the type of weapon the man carried, but he recognized death when he saw it. He dived back across the alley, skidding on his belly and ripping away both uniform and skin as he slid. He crashed hard into the wall just as the pavement erupted in a black geyser of molten plastic.

"Down the alley," he ordered Trahnee. "They'll kill us both if you don't."

She nodded bleakly and hurried off. Norlin laid down a covering fire for her, barely avoiding the explosive-projectile weapon pointed his way. A tumble of plastic blocks from the building wall came crashing down from above his head. He nimbly avoided them then used the pile as a barricade to get off two quick shots at the rebel. One of his beams caught the man high in the forehead, sending him spinning back.

Norlin didn't hesitate. He followed Trahnee to the end of the alley and ran out into the street to wave down a passing armored truck laden with Empire Service troopers. The driver saw Norlin's sub-commander's gold meteor on his lapels. The truck slowed, and a half-dozen armed soldiers dropped from the rear. The truck sped away, leaving Norlin to face the muzzles of six laserifles.

"The skirmish is on the next street over. Not more than fifteen with explosive-projectile weapons. They're led by an Empire Service officer named Delamier." Norlin rushed on to describe the genhanced officer.

"Why are you getting involved?" demanded the squad sergeant.

Norlin started to reply, but no words came. He swallowed hard then got his wits about him.

"Why shouldn't I? I'm an Empire Service officer. I'm captain of the cruiser *Preceptor*, in dock." He turned his eyes toward the bright-blue, white-cloud-dotted sky as if he could see his vessel and the Port Authority space station.

"You're not a native?"

"I don't like your tone, Sergeant," Norlin said. The short, burly non-com looked about fifteen years older than he was and acted as if he spoke to a child.

"Kiss my ass," the man said. "Take him into custody, Desallo. We got rebels to kill."

One soldier stepped away from the others and sighted down the barrel of his rifle at Norlin.

"I'm an Empire Service officer!" Norlin raged. "You're under my command!"

"Kill him if you have to—or maybe even if you just want to," the sergeant said over his shoulder. "We don't have time for off-planet outgassers."

Desallo's finger twitched on the firing stud. Norlin turned and squarely faced him. Fighting the aliens had been hard until the last few days on Sutton II because they were unseen and unknown. Facing one of his own species intent on murdering him made him angry.

"Soldier," he barked. "Report!"

"I don't take orders from you. The sarge he said for me to burn you. He don't want prisoners. We got to answer to the civil authorities when we take prisoners. Costs too damned much to let them go to trial, and the budget won't take it any more this year. That's what the sarge says."

"You kill any rebels you capture?" Norlin asked, astounded. Porlock turned from an idyllic paradise into a bloodbath before his eyes. He began to understand why a rebellion had started if all the Empire Service troops were like these.

"Why not? They deserve it."

"They deserve a trial, no matter what it costs," Norlin said. He watched Desallo's finger tighten until it turned white. A fraction of a millimeter more and it would trigger a vortex of prodigious energy that would rip through Norlin's body as if it were nothing but a column of swirling dust.

He acted without thinking. His body turned slightly to the left. As Desallo started to follow the motion with the laserifle, Norlin blasted forward as if he had been rocket-launched. His fist smashed into the trooper's exposed throat. He felt the cartilage crush. Blood erupted from the dying man's nose and mouth. Norlin kept driving in to the attack, ducking around behind so his left arm circled Desallo's body and forced him onto his heels.

The soldier was dead by the time he hit the pavement. Norlin ripped the laserifle away from the lifeless fingers and stood over the man, panting. The exertion had been slight, but the emotional strain of killing a man with his bare hands had taken a toll. At the Empire Service Academy, he had been taught unarmed combat and had always wondered why. He meant to become a spaceman, the captain of a powerful cruiser. He would kill from distances measured in light-minutes and seldom see the result.

He forced himself to look away from the dead soldier. More important priorities drove him now.

"Trahnee!" he called. The genhanced woman was nowhere in sight. He cursed, knowing she had abandoned him to return to Bo Delamier. She and the officer might bring this revolt to a successful end if all Empire Service soldiers treated the populace as badly as the squad he had confronted.

Another Empire Service vehicle swung around the corner. This one sported an ugly energy weapon snout on the roof of the cab. Norlin imagined the radar tracking beam bouncing off his body and racing back at the speed of light to a small on-board computer that identified him as an enemy. He dived just as the energy cannon blasted a deep pit in the street behind him.

Rolling, he came to his feet and ran for his life. The sound of pursuit died as he kept cutting through alleys and seeking out the smallest passageways possible.

When he finally came to a halt, he had no idea where he was. Looking around turned him even bleaker. The once-lovely and peaceful city had sprouted tongues of flame from the buildings housing the pleasure palaces. The revolt had begun in earnest—and he was trapped in the middle, a target for both sides.

Chapter Twelve

Pier Norlin sat in a small room staring out the broken window into the street. Under other circumstances, he would have enjoyed the view. The golden-paved street wandered in graceful curves down to a lakefront where gentle waves lapped at shimmery white sand. In the lake, fish broke the surface, creating silvered circles in the sunlight radiating outward to infinity. The breeze coming through the shattered ragged plastic windowpane carried on it the soft scents of spring and the promise of a summer filled with unspoken delights.

It was almost impossible for him to believe this delicately crafted, well-designed building facing the park and lake stood in the center of a major city.

He ignored the smell of growing plants and concentrated on the occasional whiff of ozone from repeatedly discharged laserifles. By this scent, he hunted. Twice in the past four hours he had been ambushed by rebel bands. Twice he had fought his way free. He thought he had caught sight of Bo Delamier after the second ambush in the middle of the city, but he couldn't be sure.

He would have tracked the genhanced officer down and shot him like a beast if he had been certain of his target. Porlock V might not be the paradise its veneer suggested, but it had been closer before the rebellion against the Empire began. Norlin sympathized with the citizens over their treatment by the Empire Service officers and troops he had seen, but a criminal garrison did not mean the planet should attempt to secede from the Empire. Procedures existed for the people of any world, especially a colony world, to have Emperor Arian review the behavior of his commanders.

He squinted into the bright syrupy sunlight, waiting for the thunder of armed and armored vehicles. He had spotted an Empire Service column heading in this direction. Given the chance, he thought he could establish contact and straighten out the mistake back in the city. The sergeant had been wrong; Desallo had paid for it with his life. Norlin experienced a moment's twinge at the thought of how he had killed so easily and quickly with his bare hands, then pushed it away. The trooper's death lay on the sergeant's head.

Pier Castor Norlin was a sub-commander in the Empire Service and the captain of the Nova Class Cruiser *Preceptor*. He knew his sworn duty and would not be deterred.

At the thought of his ship, he touched the com-link at his belt and cursed anew. It might have been Delamier's doing or some clever rebel leader might have considered it a tactic worthy of trying, but he could not establish a positive link with his ship. The heavy static thwarting communication up and down the spectrum wasn't from natural causes. He had checked sunspot activity and background radiation before deciding the jamming came from somewhere on-planet.

If it continued, he would be unable to bring the *Preceptor* up to battle readiness. Even worse, he was unable to reach the others in his crew. He wondered how Gowan Liottey fared with the doctors trying to restore his brain function. If Trahnee had contacted them, they might have his first officer vivisected by now. Barse, Sarov and Miza could take care of themselves, given half a chance.

Still, he worried about their safety even as he worried about the fate of his ship. Such a powerful weapon docked above the heads of the Empire troopers would prove a strong lure for Delamier. The *Preceptor* could reduce the planet to rubble instead of defending it. With the alien radiation cannon, it could lay waste to entire worlds—just the power Delamier sought.

Norlin wished he hadn't been cut off so completely from the spaceport and his shuttle.

The whine of powerful tesla turbines alerted him to the approaching tank. He ducked down and checked the captured laserifle. Against the tank, it was a feeble weapon. If troops rode on the armored skirts, however, he had a chance to strike.

He shook himself. He was beginning to think like a rebel. He was an officer in the Empire Service. Those inside the tank were just like him—loyal to Emperor Arian. He waited for the tank to lumber into view.

Its spherical turret whirred around as sensors reached out to find any motion, any IR trace, any hint of EM radiation within its range. He cursed when he saw the side-looking synthetic aperture radar.

The powerful fighting machine could look directly through the building's walls and spot his outline.

Less than ten seconds passed before the tank's heavy lasartillery trained on the building. A voice boomed out over his com-link, garbled and almost undecipherable behind the heavy jamming static.

"Come out or we shoot."

He laid his laserifle against the wall and stood up inside the room, the upper half of his body showing through the blasted plastic window.

"I'm Sub-Commander Norlin of the Empire Service Cruiser *Preceptor*. Do not shoot!"

"Come out or we will," came the repeated command.

Norlin tensed. He didn't face a human-controlled tank but a fully automated one. Any deviation on his part from its programmed protocols would bring those awesome laser cannon into action against him.

"Do not shoot by order of Emperor Arian," he said. "I am an officer in the Empire Service." He moved to the door and stood so the sensors could fully scan his uniform. "Check my identity against your data banks. I landed less than six hours ago."

"I do not have access to such information," the tank responded.

"Take me to your commander. I order it."

"You are not my commander."

"Take me now!"

Norlin thought the turret ground back and forth in indecision. He knew that wasn't possible. He falsely attributed human characteristics to a machine incapable of vacillation. His only hope lay in convincing the expert system running the tank that he was an asset rather than an enemy. If he had the proper code words he might have succeeded. As it was, the best he could hope for was being taken to the ES commander.

He hoped the officer in charge didn't share the sergeant's opinion of taking rebel prisoners.

"You will climb aboard and sit on my front armor. My commander will speak with you. Consider yourself under protective custody until then," the tank said.

"If I am in the protection of your commander," he said, trying to force the on-board computer to relinquish some small control to him, "I am allowed to bring my own weapons." He waited. The tank did not dispute his claim. He reached inside the door and hoisted the laserifle to port arms.

Heartened by the lack of response from the tank, he marched in his best military style to the designated area and climbed aboard.

"I'm ready. Take me to your commander," he ordered.

The tank whined as its turbine pumped up to full pressure. The heavy fighting vehicle lumbered along more smoothly than Norlin would have thought as it returned to the city center. He hunkered down behind an armor-plate flange as they came to the neighborhood he had left only an hour before.

The breathtakingly designed soaring crystal towers with their supporting multi-planed flying buttresses sparkled in the sunlight. The buildings might have been constructed of precious stones, they gleamed so brightly. Beauty decreased and the signs of civil war increased as the tank rolled along the streets, turning this way and that until Norlin was confused as to direction.

He heaved a sigh of relief when he spotted a statue of the emperor and the high-rise offices with its comet-and-sun Empire logo. The tank had brought him to those who could help him most.

Norlin settled the laserifle on his shoulder and was prepared to jump off when a hint of movement at the corner of his eye caused him to swing around.

He yelled an incoherent, unneeded warning to the tank just as the laser sight locked on to the sloping metallic turret. Norlin kicked hard and got off the tank. His com-link sputtered as the tank started to order him to remain aboard; then, a nova erupted above his head.

The rebel's weapon locked on target. The projectile following the laser sighting beam blasted the turret from the tank and rained down molten steel for several minutes. The deafening roar took that long to die in Norlin's ears. He stood on weak legs behind the emperor's statue, shaking and using it for support. It had saved him from the same fate as the tank.

A burned-out hulk rested on its side. The rebel missile had been more potent than required for a medium combat tank. That knowledge chilled him. The rebels used advanced weapons capable of outgunning Empire Service light robotic tanks.

"You're a survivor, Captain Norlin," came a familiar mocking voice over his com-link. "Surrender immediately or die. I assure you it will be a pleasure to destroy you. I have turned you into the symbol of the Empire Service and everything evil it stands for. Every successful revolt requires such a target to focus hatred."

"Suck space," Norlin growled. He touched the stud on the laserifle to begin charging. He had fewer than a dozen full-energy shots in it, but that would be enough if he got Delamier sighted in properly. He shared something with Delamier. He would enjoy killing the genhanced officer as much as Bo Delamier wanted to turn him into plasma. "I don't listen to turncoats."

"How noble. Trahnee said you were an idealist. Such fools die so much more satisfactorily when executed publicly. Will you make a speech praising dear Emperor Arian? Such will resonate with the rebels and increase their determination a hundredfold."

"How did you get into power so quickly?" asked Norlin. "Why do they trust you?" He looked around, trying to home in on Delamier. The genhanced was nowhere to be seen. Using his com-link afforded him little in the way of information—the field strength of Delamier's transmission seemed uniform in all directions.

Then the genhanced officer did the unthinkable. He strode out from a building, a lasepistol dangling indolently from his fingers. Only when he reached the spot where the tank had been turned into a puddle of molten metal did he stop and look directly in Norlin's direction, as if daring him to fire.

A sneer curled his lips as he said, "I have powers you cannot possibly grasp. After all, I am genhanced. Gaining control over mere humans is quite easy for me." He threw out his arms and lifted his face to the sky as he called, "Shoot, Norlin. Cut me down. You know you want to and have ever since we met."

Coldness filled Norlin. Delamier might be crazy, but he was no fool and suicide wasn't in his nature. He was baiting him, taunting him into firing for some reason. Although he couldn't detect it, Norlin suspected some sort of damping field had been turned on that would create feedback in any energy weapon. This was, after all, Empire Service HQ, and such defenses would be standard.

He looked around for a way out. He couldn't hope to fight his way free—not easily—but he wasn't going to give up to the strutting genetic freak.

To his right lay the Empire Service building. As he studied its facade, he knew no sanctuary lay inside. Small laser-drilled holes marred the front, showing the intense fighting that had already taken place. Anyone inside would have been detected by the rebels' proximity, IR or gravimetric sights and burned instantly. He turned and looked across the broad square and saw a pair of office buildings that might house the main body of rebels. Both had glasteel windows capable of transmitting the deadly laser beams without having telltale holes burned through them.

Rumbling from behind told him that heavy armor moved in. He didn't care if it belonged to the surviving Empire Service garrison or the rebels. Either way, he would end up as a single entry in a data bank: killed in action. The rest of his record would be deleted to make room for more current, living servicemen.

"There is no escape, Norlin. Trust me."

Norlin ignored Delamier's words. He turned off the comlink, not sure if the genhanced officer could trace him using it. The rebels' capability startled him, just as it obviously had the lax Empire Service troopers.

To leave the shelter of the statue meant exposing himself to sophisticated tracking devices—Norlin found himself clinging to even the partial protection from the simpler sensors afforded by the bronze statue's mass. But he had no choice The rumble of two tanks tracking around into the square shook him from his indecision.

They trained their heavy turret weapons on the office building to his left. Norlin sucked in a deep breath and ran for his life when the first actinic bolt of laser death spat forth and lapped along the front of the structure. He skidded on his belly and wiggled into a shallow trench just as four laser beams sought his flesh. He kept kicking and struggling as the pavement blew up in towering gouts behind him.

He stopped suddenly as the pavement in front of him grew hot. He had no idea what type of weapon Delamier used against him, but it was slower acting than a laser—he might have been right about some sort of counter-field to his laserifle. Kicking free of his channel, he dashed behind one tank.

Small automated pellet weapons mounted on the tank fired at him. Their hot breaths singed his body. Norlin knew they were flesh-activated explosives when they failed to erupt as they smashed into the ground behind him. Riot control on Porlock V had turned vicious. He wondered if the garrison commander had authorized neutron bombs, too—kill the people, leave the property intact.

A portion of the paving had been rent and twisted as gases beneath the ground had blown a huge hole. Norlin dived headfirst into it, not caring what he entered. To remain on the surface meant sure death. The auto-tracking weapons on the powerful tank would home on him in seconds, and Delamier would gleefully allow them to kill one of their own officers.

Only his quick reflexes saved him.

He knew instantly he had entered a deep pit—a very deep one. He fell past a twisted girder, grabbed and almost held on. The sharp metal lacerated his hand, turning it slippery with blood. He lost his grip, but the slowing of his fall let him swing his feet around to crash into another girder. The impact jolted him, but one leg curled around the beam and held.

For several seconds, he hung upside down. The hiss of laser weapons and the ground-shaking blasts of the battle in progress above forced him to action. Straining, every muscle in his belly wanting to rupture, he pulled himself double and got his good hand on the metallic beam. Another convulsive twist brought him flat on the beam. He lay along its cool length, mind racing.

"Metal beam," he panted. "Underground support. What would they have underground on Porlock that needed such strength?"

A piercing whine from beneath gave him the answer. A high-speed transporter ferried people and cargo from one side of the world to another. Rather than scar the pristine blue skies of their world with contrails and pollution, the planetary designers had chosen to bury their necessary mass transit.

Norlin peered over the edge, knowing he had only a few more seconds of safety before either the Empire Service tanks or the rebel lasers bored down through the hole and found him. Twenty meters below stretched the superconducting tracks for the transporter. Norlin knew he couldn't survive such a drop, even though the planet's gravity was a few percent less than Earth norm.

He scooted along the beam until he found a cross member. Attached to it, a dozen meters away, hung a ladder. He heaved a sigh of relief. The local engineers conducted personal surveys of their facilities as well as letting robots check. He dropped down the ladder just as winking blue beams of coherent light cut through the opening overhead.

It didn't matter if those were tank lasers or from Delamier and the rebels. Dead was dead if one hit him. He touched the com-link at his belt, wishing the static would go away. He didn't leave it on long, fearing Delamier might trace him. Even if the Empire Service had triumphed above, Delamier had escaped. The genhanced was too wily to be caught or killed easily.

Norlin stood on the transporter track and felt the quiver of vibrant energy through the yttrium-barium-copper alloy. He looked up and down the tunnel and shivered with dread. A transporter had just passed; he hadn't seen which direction it had gone. Even worse, he had no idea what schedule the transports kept. Were they sent regularly or sporadically—and did that even matter? When the next transporter sailed through at transonic speeds became his overriding concern.

A single glance up to the small hole blown through the paved surface of the ES headquarters square showed no possible retreat. He saw an edge of tank tread. The entire vehicle shimmered with energy discharge as it fought off a laser attack, partially turning some of the beam aside along its shiny sloped sides and radiating the rest using high-speed heat exchangers. Even thirty meters below it, Norlin felt the intensity of the battle raging.

Again he touched the com-link at his belt. A single request might give him information about the tunnel and the transporter schedules. It might even stop a transporter already launched along these tracks. If he used the com-link, though, he alerted Delamier that he still lived. The genhanced officer probably had no illusions about that, but Norlin needed any advantage, no matter how slim. He pulled his hand away from the com-link and turned to his left. The darkness in either direction seemed absolute.

He had no reason but instinct for choosing this way. He walked into the gloom. Within a dozen meters, the twilight turned pitch black, darkness deeper than any he had experienced. Even in interstellar space there was some light—from stars, from his ship, from spacesuit instruments. In the transporter tunnel, he found none.

His breath came in fast, quick pants. He tried to control his breathing when he realized it wasn't exertion that caused his rapid heartbeat or shortness of breath. It was fear.

The bulk of his life had been spent inside spaceships, and not once had he felt so compressed, so constricted. A simple flip of a toggle brought up an exterior vidscreen panorama of infinite space. Here, he was unable to determine distances. Claustrophobia almost paralyzed him.

Norlin bounced from side to side, touching the walls to give dimension to his coffin. He swallowed hard and wiped sweat from his face. He had confronted the Death Fleet and not panicked like this. It didn't matter. He walked faster, his heart rising in his chest and clogging his throat.

In minutes, he was running headlong into the lightless depths of the tunnel. He began to see images moving in front of him through the darkness. Phantoms of the mind reared and clawed viciously at him.

Then he began to truly fear for his life. The hum of the superconducting rails increased.

Another transporter was en route, and he had no idea if he were running into it or it was overtaking him from behind. If it came from either direction, he would be crushed to death in a split second, surrounded by the absolute darkness.

Chapter Thirteen

The humming rails betrayed the onslaught of superconducting power. Pier Norlin ran faster—and he didn't know if he ran toward death or from it, if direction even mattered. The transporters shot through their burrows at transonic speeds.

He felt the prodigious power of the heavy machine as it caused a change in pressure along the pitch-dark tunnel. It might be fifty kilometers away and closing on him at thirty kilometers a minute.

His lifetime was measured in minutes. Less.

He ran and ran and ran until strong hands grabbed his shoulders and pulled hard. He flailed about in the darkness, struggling to get away from the hands, from the certain death offered by the transporter. He didn't know where he wanted to go. All he knew was that he had to get there soon.

"Moderate your rods, fool!" More hands gripped him, tugging at his sleeves and legs. A pair caught his right wrist. He pulled free, only to have others find his ankles. Bodily, the unseen men picked him up and tossed him aside.

He crashed against a flimsy wooden platform that sagged under his weight. He tried to sit up, but a half-dozen bodies crushed down atop him. Norlin slumped, panting for breath. Then came a curious stillness in the tunnel. A partial vacuum formed, followed by the ear-tearing shriek of the transporter ripping by.

It took several minutes for him to recover. When he did, he was partially deaf and still blind in the darkness but free of the pressure on his body. He heaved a few quick breaths and made sure he still lived.

"What happened?" he asked the darkness, not even sure if anyone was near.

A faint rustling grew in intensity until he was certain more than a dozen people watched him. His hand moved to his belt and touched the pistol holstered there. He didn't even remember losing the laserifle. That might have vanished while he still wiggled around on his belly on the surface with the two tanks and Delamier's rebels shooting at each other.

"No need to use that, consociate mine. We are all of a like mind down here."

The ringing in his ears faded more and more. Norlin turned toward the speaker. "If you're the one who rescued me, thank you."

"A pity such a fine sport of a man as you is a bit daft," said a woman in the opposite direction from the first speaker. "Even the real wobble-wobbles don't go poking around in these tunnels when the ESers are marching above. Those are troop suppliers that go on by so fast, they are."

Norlin pressed his back against the wall. From their tone, whoever had rescued him held the "ESers"—the Empire Service garrison—in low regard. He slid his hand toward his pistol then stopped. It wouldn't do him any good to start firing it blindly. They obviously outnumbered him, and equally obvious, they saw him with perfect clarity.

"Are you using IR goggles?" he asked.

"About all you'd expect an ESer to ask," grumbled someone. "You can't expect genhanced responses from their kind."

"Are you genhanced?" Norlin asked.

"What else? This is the only safe place on the whole worthless world."

That startled him. He'd always associated the dregs of society with living in the underground, subsisting on the debris of the more civilized populace. Even the craziest of the genhanced found positions in the Empire Service. They were Emperor Arian's darlings, and no behavior, no matter how outrageous, seemed out of line or couldn't be excused.

Norlin couldn't help thinking about Bo Delamier. The man had engaged in outright insurrection against the emperor at least twice, and his punishment had been command of a space station protecting one of the more valuable mining worlds in the empire. He thought that made the emperor more deranged than those serving him.

Perhaps the only mistake the rebels on Porlock's surface made was in trusting Delamier. Emperor Arian certainly had not won any trust from Norlin recently, either through action or appointment of capable officers on this world.

"We get the IR goggles from the ESers who come down here to wipe us out," spoke up another of the crowd around him. "They're not much good. Hinky over there worked up better ones one dull afternoon. They can magnify a single photon into daylight, but they suck power like a black hole."

"Try these."

Norlin felt thin, crisp wafers thrust into his hands. He turned them over as he felt them. Wires ran from the sides and an elastic band intended for holding them in place had seen better days. He slid them on, eyes screwed shut tightly.

Cautiously, he opened his eyes. The once-dark tunnel brightened until it shone as brilliantly as if the noonday sun had penetrated the meters of rock-and-steel ceiling.

"Don't go worrying over getting blind if a light flash goes off in your face. Hinky's no fool, even if he is genhanced. He built in suppressor circuits that work faster than the eye."

"Thanks again," Norlin said.

He slowly studied those arrayed around him in a half-circle. He sat on a low wooden platform built up and off the track, possibly intended for work crews to slide into safely to allow the transporter to pass. He saw scuff marks where computer controllers had rested on the wood, confirming his guess.

"What are you doing down here?" demanded the querulous woman. "We don't want your kind here."

"He might not be an ESer," the apparent leader said. Norlin couldn't make out colors, but the man stood slim, erect and carried himself with an air of one used to authority. "He might be in disguise, though it doesn't seem too likely. Uniform fits him too well. Spies always get their clothes from someone else."

"I'm the captain of an Empire Service cruiser docked at the space station," Norlin admitted. He waited for the men and women to attack him. His confession had little effect one way or the other.

"They finally called in off-world support," said Hinky. "It was only a matter of time."

"I'm here on a mission that has nothing to do with your civil war," Norlin said. He hurried on to explain about the threat posed by the aliens and their genocidal ways. Those gathered along the transporter tracks began yawning as their eyes shifted from Norlin to either side of the infinite tunnel.

"It's important to stop them. Vital to our survival! We proved they aren't invincible on Sutton," he said with heat. "We have to put aside differences or they'll wipe out all humanity."

"More power to them," Hinky said. "I sat next to Emperor Arian, and what'd it get me?" He snorted and walked off.

"Wait!"

Norlin lost the rest of his audience, in twos and threes, until only the argumentative woman and the man he thought was the leader remained.

"You speak a good vidrama piece, I'll give you that," the man said. "What goes on above the ground don't interest us much. We have other concerns."

"Eating, more than any other thing," the woman cut in. "What's for dinner, you old fool? You been wasting your time saving him and not finding us anything to eat."

"Quiet, Meli. This one's different from most of the ones blundering around down here."

"How?"

Norlin saw the argument beginning and strove to forestall it. "I need your help. Both of you," he said earnestly.

This got the woman's attention. She turned suspicious eyes on him. They looked larger than life, magnified by the goggles she wore.

"Nobody's ever said that to me. The likes of you need my help? That smacks of space dust to me."

"Porlock isn't like other planets," Norlin said. "The Empire Service on other frontier worlds protects, serves, does research and tries to explore uncharted systems." He shrugged helplessly. "Porlock V might be too close to Earth and the emperor's court. Both have turned decadent."

"It's a lovely world, it is," said the man. "I have no need to go anywhere else."

"You need my help?" the woman repeated.

"I have to contact my ship." Norlin touched the com-link at his belt.

"Not with that, you won't," Meli said. "Hinky took out all the circuitry. Don't know what he's going to use it for, but he's clever, that genhanced bastard is."

Norlin's hand shot to the com-link and pulled it free. The instant it came off the snap he knew Meli wasn't lying. The case had been carefully cracked open and the innards removed. He sagged, then straightened and smiled.

"At least Delamier can't track me."

"You want to talk to your ship up at the Port Authority?" asked the man.

"That chance is gone now." Norlin started to toss aside the empty case, then stopped. For no good reason other than habit, he snapped it back onto his belt.

"We can hop a transporter and get down 'Quator Station."

"That's where all the transporters radiate from. Like the navel of a diseased world, it is," said Meli. "Worse than that, the space station hangs direct over it."

"There are laser uplinks?" asked Norlin.

"There's more gadgets there than even Hinky can figure out. We go there time to time and scavenge. Not many people around these days when everyone's killing everyone else."

"We just get aboard a transporter and go?" asked Norlin.

"More to it than that," the man admitted. "You jump one. They don't much slow down between destinations."

"But they're traveling transonic!" Norlin couldn't believe the man meant to board a transporter while it was under full powered flight.

"Makes it more fun," Meli said. "You got agar for guts, or you want to try it?"

He wished the light intensifier allowed color highlights. All he saw was black and white with hints of color. Lost were subtle facial changes. From the woman's tone, though, she meant what she said.

"You've done it?"

"She's on every damned transporter going to Isotope City. I think she's got another lover."

"Throw yourself on the rails if you think that, Skeggon. You're outgassing and you know it!"

"She might," the man /insisted.

"How do you get on the transporter?" asked Norlin.

"Come along for the ride, and I might show you. None of this jetting back if you get scared."

"It's for the wobble-wobbles, even if Hinky invented it," said Skeggon.

Norlin didn't have any idea how they managed to jump onto a streamlined cargo machine travelling more than twenty-five hundred kilometers per hour, but he didn't have to be crazy to try. Desperation pushed him to try anything, even if it was "for the wobble-wobbles."

"Come along. Not far. You coming, too, Skeggon?" asked Meli.

"You go. Be back before dinner. I'm hijacking an ESer food transport, I am."

"And I'm my own grandmother!" shot back Meli. "Damned coward. Come along now, and let me show you the drill for getting to 'Quator Station and no one being any the wiser."

Norlin followed her down the tunnel. He kept touching the rail warily, expecting it to hum and signal the approach of another transporter.

"How long do we have to wait?" he asked, feeling nothing unusual in the superconducting rail.

"We find a cross tunnel and pick up the Latitude Dropper straight to the Station. Shouldn't be more than an hour."

Norlin closed his eyes and took a deep breath. Waiting was more difficult than trying to grab on to a smooth-hulled transporter could ever be.

They walked for twenty minutes until he noticed the tunnel bent subtly. Any high-speed machine on this rail would slowly swing around and change direction. They had found the Latitude Dropper line that terminated at the equatorial station—'Quator Station—half a world away.

"Here," Meli said. "You want me to go along? I will, but I don't trust that Skeggon. He accuses me of zipping to 'Tope City when all he does is sniff around after that slut Adara. Hijack an ESer food shipment, ha! He's trying to hijack Adara!"

Norlin's hopes soared that Hinky had devised a system for coupling onto the supersonic transporter—and doing it safely. A man-sized cylinder with a mechanical grapple on the end rested between the rails. He found small bands of an electromagnet circling the cylinder. When turned on, the cylinder would be repulsed by the superconducting rails and rise.

"It whips right along, it does," confirmed Meli, "but the batteries aren't good for more than a few klicks. You got to get that hook up and under the front of the transporter. It jerks you around, but if you're up to speed you don't notice it much.

You ride until the red light blinks. Cut loose and turn on the electros again, coast to a stop and you're somewhere around the 'Quator Station."

"You mean turn on the electromagnet and *then* release the hook?"

"That's right. Always get it confused." Meli stopped and canted her head to one side. "Better get ready. I hear one coming, I do. Yes, it's the Lat Dropper, and it's going in the right direction."

Norlin squeezed into the tiny cylinder with its inadequate internal padding, made sure he had access to the simple controls and peered up through the open grill at the woman. She stared back down the tunnel in Skeggon's direction.

"Meli, thank you."

"That Skeggon. I know he's after Adara. I know it!"

She wandered off. Norlin called out to her, but the woman had vanished. He closed his eyes, then forced himself to flip the toggle on the electromagnet. The small cylinder rose and began whipping along between the rails, moving faster and faster just like a particle in a linear accelerator.

A whine drowned out his own aerodynamic sounds as the transporter overtook him. Even with his quick reflexes, Norlin almost missed the front of the transporter with the hook. He wondered how the people living underground ever managed this strange mode of hitchhiking. The jerk as the hook caught and dug into the metal front of the transporter snapped his head back. He felt bruises sprouting from impact with the thinly padded metal braces inside the cylinder.

Then he thought he'd go mad from the high-pitched whine from the transporter. He switched off his electromagnet to conserve battery power and let the more powerful machine pull him along for what seemed an eternity. Even as anxious to arrive at the Equator Station as he was, he almost missed the release warning.

The red light blinked on and off once. He came out of his sound-induced stupor long enough to hit the electromagnet toggle and retract the hook. The deceleration slammed him in the opposite direction. He cut his forehead and shoulder but didn't care. All around he saw signs of movement and light.

By the time he turned off the electro and climbed from the battered metal cylinder, he was cramped, aching and bloody. He was also excited. He had left Delamier far behind. With luck, he could activate the defensive systems on the *Preceptor* and guarantee the genhanced officer would never be able to use it against the Empire Service troops on-planet.

Norlin smiled. He could wrest control from Delamier in a matter of minutes with a single well-chosen remote command.

He hurried along the tunnel and came to the lighted area. Dozens of transporters rested on their magnetic skids as robots worked to load and unload cargo containers. Norlin watched for human supervisors and saw no one to demand to know what he was doing there.

Moving quickly, he dodged through the loading docks and came to a long, wide corridor filled with heavy equipment. It took him less than ten minutes to find the main control room for the shipping complex. He'd expected to use his pistol to get inside; it was deserted.

He slipped into the control room and cautiously investigated. On a computer console vidscreen, he found a recall bulletin ordering all personnel to leave the system on automatic and abandon the station. Norlin frowned, then decided Delamier had succeeded in blocking transportation of Empire Service troops and supplies. No one had the authority to override the automatic status without being present in the control room.

That wasn't his concern. He found a communications unit and studied it for several seconds. Unlike those aboard the *Preceptor*, this one was simple to use. He punched in his access code, expecting to get the computer onboard his ship.

The voice answering his coded command startled him.

"Is that you, Captain Norlin?"

"Liottey?"

"Yes, sir. Whom did you expect?"

Norlin had expected no one—or anyone else except his first officer. "What's happened? Why are you at the controls?"

"I am in command of the *Preceptor*, of course. We are in the middle of an emergency, sir. Chikako just sighted a Death Fleet scout at the system perimeter. We are launching in pursuit of the alien vessel within the hour."

"Not without me!" Norlin shouted. He quieted. "Let me speak with Barse."

"I am sorry, sir. I had to incarcerate her for insubordination. She is in the brig."

"What brig? She's the engineer. How can you go after an alien ship without an engineer?" Norlin's worst fears surfaced. Liottey had escaped the doctors supposed to be healing his CoolinGas-damaged brain and gotten back to the ship.

"Sir, I am busy with preflight checklists."

"Sarov, Miza, report."

"I am sorry, sir. Those circuits are forbidden for use during enemy engagement. Your orders."

"I'm issuing new orders. Put me through to Sarov!"

"Com silence is now in effect," Liottey said tendentiously. "We shall report when the alien ship is destroyed."

"Liottey!" screamed Norlin. The com-link went dead. He sagged back, envisioning his command being destroyed by a maniac.

Chapter Fourteen

Pier Norlin screamed into the dead circuit. Liottey had cut the com-link and gone into combat status.

"They didn't cure him. He's still crazy," he moaned. He leaned back and wiped sweat off his forehead. He felt so helpless on-planet. He should never have let Trahnee talk him into the shore leave for either himself or the *Preceptor*'s crew. They had a job to do, duty to perform, oaths to fulfill.

The Death Fleet had to be defeated.

Even more to the point, he had allowed his entire crew to ground into the middle of a civil war. He should have checked planet-side conditions before foolishly leaving his command. He should have left more automatic safeguards on the *Preceptor*. He should have done a million other things rather than pursue the imprudent course he had.

Norlin swung about and looked at the vidscreens showing the loading activity going on around him. Robots worked without human supervision as they scattered materiel across the face of the world. They didn't care about aliens or civil war. All they knew lay within their programming. They followed it; they were content.

He snorted. Could a machine ever be content? He didn't know. What he did know was that he was no machine, and he was intensely dissatisfied with the way fate treated him. Under Empire Service regulations, he was liable for court martial for dereliction of duty because he was the captain of the *Preceptor*. Gowan Liottey should never have been given the opportunity to take the cruiser into battle if the logged ranking line officer was physically and mentally capable of command.

Norlin knew what others in his position would do. To cover themselves, they would assert Liottey had mutinied. Better to blame a single renegade officer than be thought incompetent.

"It's all my fault. I should never have brought down my entire crew." He snorted in disgust again. The only permanent member of his crew to remain aboard had been the ship's cat.

The incongruity of it struck him, and he fought back a chuckle. "Maybe Neutron will generate enough methane to gas Liottey into bringing back my ship."

That thought faded as his attention turned to more immediate problems. Liottey was taking his command into battle and might not return—*would* not, unless the rest of the crew functioned as a unit. With Barse locked up somewhere, Norlin gave the *Preceptor* almost no chance of surviving an encounter with even the smallest ship in the alien's exploratory fleet.

His fingers worked the control console. Information trickled to his brain, almost of its own accord. He knew he had come to the heart of Porlock. From the 'Quator Station came and went this world's supplies. How could he turn that to his advantage?

"They have uplinks to the Port Authority space station. They must have cargo shuttles, too." His fingers danced over the control board, seeking the fastest shuttle available. He didn't think he could reach the *Preceptor* before Liottey took it into deep space, but just reaching the space station might be enough to keep him from being too harsh on himself for being such a fool. From the Port Authority station, he would command resources Delamier could only dream of—he would control access to the planet.

Try as he might, he found no working cargo shuttles. The human crews had taken them when the evacuation order had appeared on their boards. He diverted a Robot Repair Unit to a damaged vessel to get a time-of-repair estimate and knew ten RRUs weren't likely to be enough when he saw an exterior view of the blighted craft. Its superstructure had been damaged beyond the repair capacity of all but a complete dry dock.

An hour of futile work exploring the complex exhausted him. He sank to the floor at the far end of the control room. Mindlessly, the superconducting transporters came and went. He no longer tried to stop the flow of important supplies to the major population centers. Let the rebels take them. Let the Empire Service troopers seize what they could. It had turned into a moot point with him who won control for the planet. Both sides shot first and never bothered asking questions.

For the first time since this madcap adventure began, Pier Norlin closed his eyes and thought, really *thought*, about all that had happened.

"Why did I let Trahnee convince me to even come to this system?" he asked aloud. When he was with her, she stirred feelings inside him. She had used him, he knew, to get Delamier onto the planet to seize control of the rebellion. Even worse, she had insisted on vacating the *Preceptor* to remove it as a threat to Delamier's bid for power. And he had let her.

"It sounded plausible," he said to himself. "Liottey needed a doctor. Barse and the others hadn't been on R-and-R for months. I should have stayed aboard my command." Even as he spoke, he knew he couldn't have done that. The subtle tugging of the woman's soft voice would have pulled him away. She held sway over him to a degree he found uncomfortable. And unnatural.

Why? He thought he loved her. It was both as simple and as complicated as that.

She'd betrayed him to Delamier, and he still loved her.

"Enough of that. How do I get myself out of this?" He heaved himself to his feet and stalked back and forth in the control room, finally settling down in front of the master computer. He worked diligently to get a laser radar pattern of sky traffic on a vidscreen. When he did, he cursed.

"Death Fleet ships! Two elements coming toward the planet…fast." He tracked them, at first with apprehension as they neared, then with a growing confusion. Unless the 'Quator Station's lidar malfunctioned, one alien ship had just fired on the other.

Norlin tracked them until he reached a point on the horizon where needed ground units were damaged, and he lost the two vessels as they came into orbit.

"You are obsessed with them, aren't you, Pier?" came the soft, compelling voice he remembered only too well. He spun. Trahnee stood at the entrance to the control room, one long-fingered hand resting easily on her outthrust hip. His heart leaped into his throat, and he found it hard to respond.

"I didn't mean to startle you so," she said. The tall, dark-haired woman glided gracefully into the room as if moving on ball bearings rather than feet. Her grey eyes darted across the panel, appraising all the work he had done. She shook her head in amazement at what he had accomplished in such a short time. "You are so competent."

"For a mere human," he said, the harsh words burning away the shock of seeing her.

"Even for a genhanced, dear Pier. You are amazing."

"What do you want?" He wondered if he could draw his pistol—and use it.

"You, Pier. I still don't know how you got away from Bo. He's really quite furious with you over that. He worked hard to entangle you in his web."

"He said he had turned me into the focal point for the rebels to hate."

"More than that, really," Trahnee said, as if they discussed the weather. "The rebels see you as an invading menace brought by the Empire Service to further the tyranny so rampant here. The Empire Service officers think you're a turncoat."

"Like Delamier."

"Yes, like Bo." Trahnee chuckled. "I'm not sure if he shouldn't change sides and return to the Empire Service ranks. He's been very adroit constructing the lies and counter-charges needed to power the rebellion so far. Turning against his current allies might elevate his position with the ES and thereby bring him favorably to the emperor's attention again."

"I'm so happy for him." He didn't try to conceal his sarcasm.

"He has come so close before, but conditions changed on him—and he misjudged his support both times. Not now, not on Porlock. He will soon be planetary governor."

"Don't you mean dictator?"

"Please, Pier." Trahnee sounded truly aggrieved at his refusal to rejoice in Delamier's victory. "We genhanced are *supposed* to rule. It is Emperor Arian's sorry policy of nepotism that has kept Bo from his destiny thus far."

Norlin turned his attention back to the control boards. Other indicators winked at him. It might be several minutes before the alien ships reappeared over the horizon where he could track them. He found certain restricted com-link channels more interesting. The Empire Service had emergency communications capability built into the transporter station's circuits.

He barely listened to Trahnee as he worked on the circuitry. He found the code switch and thought hard. Somewhere in the back of his mind, he teased at memories of the communications class he had taken at the Empire Service Academy.

"Standard," he muttered. It came back in a flash. He tapped in a standard code his instructing officer had mentioned in passing as being in use on certain frontier worlds.

"You've opened the com-link to all the Empire Service field units," Trahnee marveled.

"So it seems." Norlin studied the new images racing across the vidscreen at the far end of the room. A small display showed the tactical positions; the larger portion of the vidscreen gave him precise activity on a phalanx of medium-armor combat tanks, likely to be as powerful as anything on the planetary surface.

"They're moving against Bo's position," Trahnee said in a hushed voice. "You can reach them, can't you? You can communicate with each unit?"

"I can control them," Norlin said, realization of his true power dawning on him. "Those are robot units. From here I can program them any way I want." He was startled to find that he *did* have command, since no other transmission reached the robot fighting machines.

"Pier, you don't owe the Empire Service anything. What have they ever done for you? They've sent you on a fool's errand. No one can fight this Death Fleet singlehandedly, yet they want you to. Are they supporting you? No!"

"No," he said. "That reminds me." He turned his attention back to the laser radar tracking unit. In seconds, both alien ships appeared on the screen. The only lidar working was centered at 'Quator Station.

"Death Fleet ships?"

"Yes," he said, fascinated. He didn't understand what had happened in the near-planet orbit. One ship chased the other, apparently trying to destroy it. "That one, the lead ship. It's going to crash about six hundred klicks away. The other one is still firing on it."

Norlin hardly heard Trahnee's gently hypnotizing comments. He touched one control after another until he got the response he desired. The emergency communications circuit didn't allow him to command the planet's limited lasartillery—he wasn't even sure if a pleasure world such as Porlock V had any—but he could reach the Port Authority space station.

Working quickly, he sent the complex attack scheme he had worked out. He smiled wryly. Much of the firing pattern had been worked out by the *Preceptor*'s one-time commander, the genhanced Captain Pensky. He and Sarov had added touches to it, making the firing order even more important.

Almost twenty seconds passed as he sent the program up to the space station.

"You're trying to destroy them!"

"Just the attacking ship," Norlin said. He watched in satisfaction as the small control he exercised over the space station's limited lasartillery worked perfectly. The heavy laser cannon caught the alien ship and blew it into debris. The lidar tracked fourteen larger pieces as they fell through the atmosphere. He didn't bother with the smaller. The ship had died within seconds of being fired upon.

"You successfully defended the planet," Trahnee said, her voice husky and her touch on his shoulder warm. "Now perform a true service. Set the tanks against their masters. Crush the Empire Service garrison. Help Bo, and we can rule this world together!"

Norlin swayed, momentarily dizzy. Her words struck him like physical blows, each taking away a bit more of his stamina and determination. Hands trembling, he reached out and began sending his new program to the automated tanks.

Chapter Fifteen

"You are so strong, Pier," Trahnee cooed. She stroked his arm as he worked on the control console. The program he sent to the Empire Service tanks hummed and whirred through the intricate electronic maze before uplinking to the space station and then returning to the ground.

The ponderous tanks moved into new formations, their deadly laser-bristled turrets swinging about seeking targets.

"You won't regret joining us. Bo and I—" Trahnee stopped speaking when she saw the vidscreen. She jerked away, her mouth forming an O. No words came out. Her horror was too great.

"Delamier will be lucky to escape with his life," Norlin said. He wiped sweat from his forehead. He had wanted to join the rebellion with all his heart, to turn his back on his oath of duty and all that he held sacred. He had no love of Emperor Arian. He had seen what the man's cruel and often capricious rulings had done across the frontier. The worlds along the star frontier crumbled and fell away from the Empire forever, due both to the emperor's uncaring dictates and the action of the Death Fleet.

Still, Norlin knew that humanity would die in the cold darkness of space unless the Empire Service held the worlds together in some semblance of a union. The aliens would pick them off one by one if they didn't.

Yet Trahnee's words had struck him so hard he still shivered in reaction. What was her hold on him? Love? It had to be more than that.

"You—" She sputtered incoherently, still not believing he had betrayed her and sent the tanks against the rebel positions.

"The battle is over," Norlin said, tired to the core of his being. "The rebels are wiped out."

"The *war* isn't over," she said, her voice quavering. "Bo isn't dead. He's too wily for that. He is too good a commander to die with his men. There's no way he could fight again if he died."

"It will take him time to regroup," Norlin said. "By then I should have authorization patched through the main Empire Service computers. This is makeshift." He thanked his attentiveness at the Academy for that chance hearing of the code required to take temporary command. "I wish Delamier would stop his civil war, because we need to work against the aliens. We only make it easier for them to destroy us all."

"Is that how you resist me?" Trahnee asked. "You fixate on the damned aliens?"

"Resist?" Norlin slumped in the command chair and stared at her. Did he love her? Possibly. Probably. But her words sparked other lines of thinking.

She showed none of the capabilities other genhanced did—that he noticed. Her words indicated astonishment at his ability to deny her.

Norlin began to understand Trahnee—and her talent. And the menace she posed.

"You are remarkable," she said. "But enough of this. You must—"

"No!" Norlin sat upright in the chair, hands gripping the edge of the panel. "You might control Delamier, but you aren't controlling me. I have work to do."

"Pier, my darling..."

"Don't start on that." He angrily denied any feelings for her. He no longer knew if they were honest love, lust, or emotions induced by her lilting, hypnotic voice. She influenced subtly and rose to power by standing behind others. Norlin had no doubt she had incited Delamier to rebellion on the other worlds. The genhanced officer's tactical ability was great; Norlin had seen that. What Delamier lacked in ambition, Trahnee supplied for him.

"I need to contact the *Preceptor*," he said. "Liottey has taken control. What clinic did you send him to?" he demanded. "I have to find out if the therapy had even begun."

"I turned him over to the Port Authority doctor at the field. I know little about such things except that they are good and could help him."

Norlin began working through the single Empire Service circuit he had opened, trying to access data banks, monitor the progress of the tanks, checking periodically with the Port Authority space station to see if elements of the Death Fleet had been sighted—and if the *Preceptor* had tried to contact the base.

He failed on all counts. Even worse, he wasn't able to pinpoint the alien ship's crash site. He needed a dozen others helping gather such intel. He needed his crew, and Liottey had them under his control on a suicide mission.

"Pier," came Trahnee's soft, meek voice. "I located the hospital where they worked on your first officer." She stepped back and let him see the information parading across the vidscreen. He absorbed it in a flash. Fingers working expertly, he linked to the clinic.

A pleasant man smiled at him from the vidscreen.

"How may we be of assistance, sir? Has someone in your command experienced life-threatening injuries? Allow the Mentin Clinic to provide exclusive medical support for you."

"I've already had an officer in your care," Norlin said, startled at the sales pitch. On many worlds the Empire Service had to contract for medical support. "Gowan Liottey. Coolin-Gas accident that damaged his neurochemical balance."

"Ah, yes, Lt. Liottey. An easy cure and quick recovery, thanks to the Mentin Clinic's exclusive advanced healing techniques. He tested within one sigma of his norm and was released."

"Is paranoia possible after his therapy?" Norlin asked, still not reassured. Liottey didn't have the nerve to imprison Tia Barse. Not in his normal state.

"There are some contra-indications to our therapeutic regimen," the pleasant, smiling man answered. It finally occurred to Norlin that he was speaking to a computer simulation and not a real person. Although this happened often, it irritated him unduly. Too much hung in the balance for cheery conversation with a machine.

"Paranoia?"

"Megalomania. He may have exaggerated faith in his abilities for a few months. These are transient problems and of no consequence."

"Did you give him an up-check to return to duty?"

"Of course. All three officers on the cruiser demanded it. We gave full approvals to Sarov, Miza and Barse, according to our records."

"Damn." Norlin switched off, angry. The clinic had discharged a patient capable of destroying the world. He supposed they were lucky not knowing what they had done, granting the release. Liottey wanted only to take on the entire Death Fleet. In his attempt, he would take Norlin's ship and command with him.

"I'm sorry, Pier. Truly I am."

"Yes, I'm sure you are." Norlin closed his eyes and tried to relax. He couldn't. A thick vein throbbed in his forehead. He started to pull away when Trahnee came to him and gently rubbed his temples.

"Relax, Pier, darling. Relax and listen only to my words."

He fought the hypnotic effect, but the genhanced woman did nothing more than urge him to rest tired, tensed muscles. He felt the tension seeping from him like pressurized gas from a leaky transfer line. His confidence in himself returned, and refreshed, he opened his eyes.

Battle positions snapped into his mind, crystal clear. He knew every possible move and the counter for it. The rebels had been defeated, and he had guided the Empire Service forces to victory.

He shook himself. He knew how to win. He had to issue the orders.

Pushing away from Trahnee, he began simulation work on the computer. The facilities were not equal to his needs. He had to issue commands to the tanks and the few remaining Empire Service ground troops without first projecting battle results in a computer.

"You're doing well," she said, and he knew that he was. His confidence soared. All he needed to do was put the final touches to the attack. How the rebels had come to power was obvious. Equally clear was the method to stop them—and Bo Delamier.

Norlin worked frantically on the computer console, his eagerness to get the orders transmitted overwhelming him. Not for the first time, he wished for a voice command circuit. On-planet they were common, since there was little chance for atmospheric loss. Such a circuit would have tripled his efficiency.

In the end, it didn't matter. He leaned back and watched the tactical positions of the tanks slowly spreading across his vidscreen. The reports buoyed his good spirits.

"The rebels are finished," he said. "There might be a few pockets of resistance, but the garrison can handle them."

"You purposefully killed off certain elements of your own forces," Trahnee accused. "Why did you do that?"

"There aren't many line officers left," he admitted. "They didn't know their orders weren't coming directly from Empire Service headquarters." He paused to put his thoughts into a more coherent stream. He had killed off many men needlessly.

"The new order on Porlock won't make the same mistakes, will they?" she asked. "You used Bo to clean out the corrupt officers taking advantage of their position."

"There aren't many above the rank of lieutenant left," he admitted. "I'm sure some innocent, capable officers died. For that, I'm sorry."

"You need not apologize to me," she said. "I instigated the rebellion."

"As you'd done twice before," he said, his pale-violet eyes squarely on her. She didn't flinch.

"Yes," she said without hesitation. "Bo is capable, but he is like a missile without guidance. He needs spin stabilization to keep him on course—to find the target at all." She knelt beside him on the floor. "You cannot know how it is at Emperor Arian's court."

Norlin wasn't sure he wanted to know how it was. From all the woman had told him, he was content living on the edge of civilization away from such decadent politics.

"There is so little to do. It is boring! For all the prattling I do about the emperor's court, I hated every instant of it. Every move is ordained. Ritual is everything. Deviation from accepted behavior is punished. And everyone is so damned smart!"

"There seems no lack of deviant behavior at the court," Norlin accused.

"That is part of what Arian enjoys so. He likes to humiliate people. He refuses to see ordinary humans. He surrounds himself only with genhanced, all vying for his attention and doing terrible things to curry his favor. How I hated it!"

He felt her passion and anger and knew it was not projected through her genhanced talent, whatever that might be. Norlin reached out and touched her gently. Trahnee turned her head to one side, catching his hand between shoulder and cheek. She twisted around slightly and kissed his hand.

"You are so different, Pier. You feel my urging but don't respond unless you want. How do you resist? No one else can."

"Is this why you were exiled from Emperor Arian's court?"

"His chamberlain discovered my talent. When I refused to aid him, he tried to have me killed. Escaping to the frontier worlds was my only chance for survival."

"What about Bo? Why did he follow you when he could have stayed?"

"Bo's my brother." Her voice hardened. "At court, we were more. Since leaving, we have…drifted apart."

Norlin recoiled involuntarily. The genhanced woman laughed at him, and this time her tone was cold, harsh, bitter.

"It's not uncommon," she said. "Arian enjoys it. He even wanted us to marry. 'Join the family's talents permanently,' he said. For all the good he could do if he wanted, he makes life miserable for his genhanced court."

"You were lovers?"

"Of course. Does that bother you? It shouldn't."

It bothered Norlin a great deal. He detected none of the urgings in the woman's voice that manipulated and caused him to veer toward action he opposed. She spoke frankly, and without putting even a patina of decency on her actions. Because of this honesty, he found his respect for her growing. He might not like what Trahnee had done, but he could admire her forthrightness.

He turned to the computer board to cover his confusion over what he felt for the woman. Love still lingered and mixed with admiration, yet revulsion battled into his brain and heart because of what she had confessed.

He finished the programming to assure the tanks achieved complete victory. He keyed a voice circuit, checked to be sure it was secure and not likely to cut out and said, "This is Captain Norlin of the Cruiser *Preceptor* congratulating you on your victory. Assemble at Empire Service HQ and re-form the chain of command."

Small red dots popped into existence on the vidscreen, showing where scattered acknowledgements began trickling into the central computer. He had no idea if the ES computer responded. It didn't matter much. The lower grade officers would soon have the situation in hand. He could do little more for them.

Except for one thing.

A flashing red star marked Bo Delamier's position. Two small tanks tracked the man as he fled through the central section of the city, seeking refuge—or escape.

"What are you going to do to Bo?" Trahnee asked.

"What do you want me to do?"

"I can't stop you," she said. He thought he caught a touch of the lie in her words, or perhaps it was only uncertainty about her inability to influence him. "I hope you'll spare him."

Norlin keyed the voice circuit again and was relieved to see that it remained active.

"Commander Bo Delamier is thought to be injured and at the following map coordinates." He read off Delamier's location. If the genhanced officer fought, he might die. If he surrendered and confessed, they might hold him for trial. Norlin suspected Delamier would respond quickly and claim to be a hero, having done what he could to defeat the rebels by infiltrating their ranks.

"Thank you," Trahnee said simply.

"He's getting more than he deserves. If he lies fast enough, he might even get a medal instead of a trial for treason."

"Bo is clever when it comes to self-preservation."

Norlin cursed. The Empire Service corps slowly regained control of their world. He lost his single command circuit as higher-priority ones superceded it. Struggling to maintain the com-link with the Port Authority space station, he sent what might be a last request for deep space tracking data on the *Preceptor*.

The space station responded quickly enough. Two lidar units reported an engagement.

"Your ship?" asked Trahnee, looking over his shoulder at the new vidscreen display.

"The *Preceptor* and the single alien vessel opposing it. There might be a chance for the ship to survive."

"What is that?" Her fingers dug into his shoulder as the computer simulation furnished bright green rays radiating from one vessel.

"Radiation cannon," he said dully. "Rapid fire. The alien is homing in on my ship."

Norlin's gut churned as he watched the vidscreen display. The alien ship swung around and fired its deadly weapon repeatedly. Where there had been two small dots indicating spaceships, there quickly became only one.

"The alien just destroyed my ship," he said in a voice almost too low to be heard.

A single red dot swung about its axis and prepared for a trajectory to Porlock. The Death Fleet's scout would be orbiting above their heads in a matter of hours—and the planet lay helpless to fend off the attack now that the *Preceptor* had been destroyed.

Chapter Sixteen

Pier Norlin stared numbly at the vidscreen display. The insignificant winking red dot creeping back toward Porlock had destroyed his cruiser.

His fingers worked on the computer console, but too much of the power he had usurped had reverted to the Empire Service headquarters when backup systems reasserted themselves. He had been lucky to find a single command circuit buried in the 'Quator Station's dispatch computer that allowed him to continue monitoring deep space radar. For this, he gave thanks. He had saved the planet from being taken over by rebels ill-equipped to fight the Death Fleet when it came.

But the hollowness inside refused to go away as he stared at the incoming ship. It had destroyed the *Preceptor* and marooned him forever on this world. He knew nothing of the alien piloting the vessel, but he hated him with an increasing passion that burned away the emptiness over the loss of his ship.

"They won't get by with this. We fought them on Sutton. We can fight them here and win."

"Always the aliens. They can't be that bad, Pier."

"You saw what they did to Renfro II. How can you say they aren't bad? They swoop down and destroy all life on a planet, loot it and then shift away to do it again on another unprepared world."

"Renfro wasn't much of a world," Trahnee said. "As to life, what did we care about the miners? There were so few of them and they were always so..." The word didn't form on her lips.

"Dirty?" Norlin finished her sentence with all the anger that had built inside. "They didn't matter because they grubbed in the dirt alongside their robot mining machines to mine rare earths necessary to keep the empire functioning?"

"No, that's not what I meant. Not exactly. They weren't...like us."

"They weren't genhanced, you mean." He swung from the woman and began working at the computer, vainly trying to make contact with Empire Service HQ. They had to turn their lasers from protecting their backs toward the stars. In its current state of disorder, Porlock would fall easy prey to the alien fleet.

"Can I help?" Trahnee asked.

"No." Norlin gave up, slumping in the chair. The com-link circuits in and out of HQ were jammed with thousands of communications. All he could do was put a message into the queue to be read whenever the new commander got around to it. Lacking the proper flag codes, he couldn't even assure his message of a conspicuous position among those vying for attention.

"I have to go to HQ and see the new commander. My rank will get me through. How many other cruiser captains are there on this world?"

"Bo might be able to help," suggested Trahnee. "He'll be at the center, trying to consolidate his position."

Norlin slumped even more. If what she said was true—and he knew it was—Delamier would be more than happy to see him. Delamier would also shuttle him off to a windowless room to be sure he never saw the light of day again. Norlin had thwarted the man in his bid to take over the planet.

Three losses wouldn't make Bo Delamier a happy man. After all, he was genhanced.

Norlin looked up and saw the alien craft changing course slightly, going into a low-energy Hohmann orbit to intersect Porlock. He marveled that the alien's tactics were those *he* would have chosen—mathematics and physics dictated so much of space travel. Even the aliens didn't have an infinite amount of energy to waste returning to the attack. Everything they did was done with cold, calculating efficiency, to make the most of their planetary looting.

"I have so much power at my fingertips," he said, "and none of it does me any good. I can send transporters anywhere in the world from this nexus point. Food? That warehouse holds anything you'd need to feed a continent. Spare parts? Electronics? RRUs? I have them all around me. A few quick commands on this board, and the transporters are sailing across the world to supply what is needed."

He slammed his hand down on the board and stood, leaning forward and breathing heavily.

"I have all that power, and it isn't good for a damned thing! I need a ship. I need to fight the aliens. All I have are transporters."

"Pier, calm yourself. You cannot think at maximum efficiency being so angry."

Trahnee touched his forehead. He started to shove her away. What did she know? She was uncaring and thought nothing of killing off a few million humans because she was genhanced and they weren't. She might as well be of the same race as the aliens for all the compassion she showed toward the colonists of the frontier worlds.

Norlin started to push free, then stopped. Her touch *did* calm him. The woman's talent lay in influencing others. How she did it was beyond his guessing. A mild form of telepathy might account for it, although the sonic content in her voice seemed more likely. He could resist because he knew her secret.

Only in darkness did Trahnee's power grow. He wondered if Bo Delamier had any inkling how his sister had manipulated him over the years. Or did the genhanced officer even care? Their goals and ambitions were probably identical.

"Relax," she urged.

He felt his tense muscles obeying the soft command until he had his anger under control and thought more clearly.

"Why not?" he said aloud. "It makes sense."

"What?" she asked.

Norlin didn't bother answering her. His fingers flashed across the board with renewed purpose, and he got as precise a location as possible for the downed alien craft. It had crashed, and he doubted much remained. But hope blossomed when he thought of it. There might be enough fire left in the engine to get into space once more.

It didn't matter if the hull had been breached—he wouldn't want to suck the alien gas mixture in any case. He could wear his spacesuit as he rode the engine into orbit. After all, he didn't need much more than that to reach the Port Authority, work out a wild scheme about how he would fight and go after the incoming alien ship before it attained orbit. He might limp into the center of the Death Fleet then set off a nuke. Taking more than a few of the alien warships with him might not be possible, but thinking about it gave him a sense of purpose.

He wasn't going to die on the ground. He was a spaceman and wanted to die defending humanity in space.

"Pier, please. What are you doing? Tell me." Trahnee stood back a pace as he ordered a transporter filled with the equipment he'd need. He knew there wouldn't be any nuclear devices stored at 'Quator Station. If they even had any on the world, such explosive devices would be under careful Empire Service guard. Still, he found enough fissionable material waiting for transport to suffice.

He couldn't make an efficient nuclear weapon, but he could make a messy one. If he sneaked into the center of the Death Fleet, he might do more than destroy a ship or two. The radioactive dust he intended to spew outward might contaminate sensitive communications equipment. If nothing else, the radioactive dust would be a marker that might activate sensors in other systems and warn of the approaching fleet.

If it didn't, it would at least prove annoying to them. Norlin had to do something to get back at the aliens for destroying his ship.

The robot handlers hummed into service on the docks as they loaded plastic crates onto a cargo transporter he had pulled from regular service.

"Where are we going?"

"*You're* returning to the city and are going to find Bo. Tell him the aliens are grouping for an attack and that I've spotted three of them so far. The rest of the Death Fleet is on its way.

He'll have to defend the world. Without the *Preceptor*, no one is leaving this time. He has to fight or die."

"There must be other ships at the Port Authority," she said, obviously intending to leave Porlock immediately.

Norlin bent over and flipped a toggle. "Port Authority, please report on docking bay status. How many ships do you have waiting for departure?"

"None," came back the answer. "This is a slow time. We're not expecting another cruise ship for a week or more."

"It might as well be a century," Norlin said as he toggled off. "There's no running this time. We win. Anything less is an alien victory."

"You have such a dramatic flair, Pier. There is always another way." She seemed too confident for him to argue. Perhaps the genhanced thought of themselves as supermen in all respects. Norlin, however, had work to do, and he was far from being a superman.

"Take the next transporter back to the city. You've only got a few minutes before it leaves."

"What are you going to do? I don't want to leave you." The way she spoke made him believe her. Tiny doubts crept into his mind, though. Was this her subtle talent for convincing him to do what she wanted, or was it a real emotion struggling to get past her barriers?

"Go on," he said gently. He escorted her down to the transporter platform. She started to protest. He pushed her toward the open door and said, "Hurry, Trahnee. I'll see you soon enough."

Her grey eyes locked with his violet ones. She shook her head sadly.

"You are planning something dangerous, Pier, my darling. But you, of all people, might be able to survive." She bent and kissed him with a mounting passion that took his breath away.

Norlin gasped as she broke off the kiss and spun into the transporter. The door cycled shut, and the transporter dropped down on the superconducting rails before he could think of anything to say.

He checked the special transporter unit he had outfitted with the material from the 'Quator Station's warehouse facilities and nodded in satisfaction that the large cargo bay was already full. He added two Robot Repair Units to the cargo then checked the programming on the transporter. It would stop at a terminus not far from the alien ship's crash site.

This was the best Norlin could hope for. If the scout ship had survived its landing intact, which he doubted, he had a way of taking the fight to the Death Fleet. Otherwise, his RRUs would have to get the ship into as spaceworthy a condition as possible. With the heavy lead canisters of plutonium and other fissionables he had loaded into the cargo bins, he would show the aliens what it meant to tangle with a human.

Pier Norlin got aboard and pressed the transit switch. The machine shuddered with energy and raced off in a different direction from that taken by Trahnee's transporter.

***

"We've got 'em in our sights!" cried Liottey. "Sarov, can you take out the alien?"

"You have us out of position. Transfer control to my board. Let Chikako and me do our jobs. You're going to get us all killed if you don't."

"I am captain of the *Preceptor*," Liottey said indignantly. "I will not relinquish command."

"Then let Barse out of that cabin where you welded her in," said Chikako Miza. "This isn't an exercise set up in our computers. The alien is going to slice and dice us and then turn us into plasma if we make any mistakes."

"Tend to the communications, Sub-Commander." Liottey sat in the command chair, his arms crossed over his thin chest. His sandy hair fell forward into his eyes. He pushed it back, not even glancing at the heads-up display forming centimeters in front of him. A simple twist of his head would give him any readout he wanted. He preferred to concentrate on the life support systems.

"I want to register a complaint, also, Gowan," said Mitri Sarov. "Where's the log so I can enter everything about this engagement?"

"Log? It's in the computer."

Gowan Liottey didn't realize Sarov had used this/his inquiry as a ploy to rise from his board and cross the control room. Liottey turned just as red warning lights flashed in his display. He had set up a defense perimeter around the command chair to warn him if anyone approached, but he had been too occupied with oxygen levels to pay full attention to Sarov's intentions.

A meaty fist lashed out and caught him squarely in the center of the chest. Liottey fell back, gagging, struggling to get air into his lungs. Warning lights flashed throughout the cabin as vital systems tied into his command chair failed.

"The son of a bitch had half the chair on a dead man's circuit. I knew I should have been more careful. Whenever anyone goes this space crazy you have to get paranoid."

"Let me help you get him out." Chikako's scalplock went dark as she unplugged from her com board and hurried to Sarov's side. She and the tactical officer dragged Liottey from the command chair. A quick look at what the first officer had done made her lips curl in disgust.

"He burned out half the control circuitry with that stunt. We can't go into battle like this. We're crippled, Mitri."

"Get Barse out of that cabin. She can fix anything."

"I'll get an RRU onto it." Chikako linked back into her board, and the lights woven into her hedge-like hair winked on and off as com traffic commenced with other parts of the ship. Liottey had barred her from any use of the com-links until this moment. She felt whole once again, even if much of the *Preceptor*'s exterior communications capability had been destroyed when Sarov knocked out Liottey.

Tia Barse shoved into the control room, her face clouded with anger.

"I'll strangle him. I'll strangle the son of a bitch and shove him feet-first into my engines. I'll turn him into atoms. Plasma! No, I'll turn him inside out and into quarks! Then I'll torture him. I swear it!"

"Sarov has him under control," said Chikako.

"He welded me into that cabin with Neutron. The damned cat outgassed the entire time. I couldn't breathe!"

"Don't feed Neutron so much protein," Chikako said. She pointed to the ruined command chair. "Liottey had it wired with a dead man's switch so that a small charge went off when Sarov slugged him. Is there any way we can get on-line before we engage?"

"Not unless we're going into battle next month." Barse's expert eye saw no chance to repair the crucial circuits without extensive work. "He might be a few bytes shy for computing but he did a job sabotaging this. Fancy that, we finally found something he was good at."

"We engage in less than fourteen minutes."

"We die in fifteen," Barse said. "And that's only if they take a full minute to attack us."

They all turned to the main vidscreen when alarms sounded. An alien ship had locked onto them and maneuvered to find the proper trajectory that would bring it close enough to a single deadly shot.

"Did he take out the radiation cannon circuits?" The readouts on the weapons panel were dead. Barse slammed her palm against the command chair, as if this might activate the damaged circuits.

"Those are intact. He didn't know what we'd done. Besides, most of it was jury-rigged and outside the usual control circuitry. The lasartillery won't function, though. I'm not sure we've got firing capability on the missiles, either. Mitri?"

Sarov grunted as he dropped into his chair and powered up the sections of his board Liottey had locked out. His bleak expression told Barse how little of the weapons system worked now that Liottey had blasted the command circuits. Sarov twisted his head this way and that as he studied his heads-up display and tried to find a way around the sabotage. More than once his concentration was broken by the approach alarm warning of the alien vessel closing on them.

"All that is left is the radiation cannon," he said. "We fight like the aliens or we don't fight at all. Unless you want to put Liottey on the hull with a sack of bolts. He can throw them at the alien scout as we flash past."

"Let's just throw Liottey at the alien," grumbled Barse. She worked personally on the command chair and then shoved free. "I'll get an RRU on this, since it requires so much work. I've got to free my circuits in the engine room and get more control of the ship back. We're going to use full power, whether we like it or not."

"No way to contact anyone about this," said Chikako. "Static is intense. Jamming from the alien. Even worse, most of my external circuits are damaged. There's nothing I can do. He took out the ranging lidar with his bomb. We're almost blind."

"I can track the alien on the CCD cameras mounted on the hull," said Sarov. "See?"

"Bad," said Barse. "This is like fighting in a bathtub. You won't be able to sight in without proper external ranging data."

"So we fire as many times as we can as fast as we can. Shotguns are old-fashioned but are still deadly at close range. We get a general position and then fire until either the alien is gone—or we are."

"You make it sound so attractive. I can hardly wait." Barse grabbed up the black cat and tucked him under her arm. She made a face as Neutron emitted another burst of methane.

Hurrying down the passageway, she stopped for only an instant to look in on Gowan Liottey. Sarov had him secured in the small surgery. An auto-med unit pumped drugs into the first officer's arm and kept him quiet. Barse didn't care what the robot doctor gave the man. If it had been left up to her, she would have chosen slow-acting poison so he would suffer like the rest of them had to.

There wasn't any point in using such a poison, however, since they were all likely to be atoms expanding at half the speed of light within a few minutes.

Seeing that Liottey posed no further problem, she rushed to the engine room and dropped the cat. Neutron stretched and then jumped onto his padded perch behind a half-dozen wrist-thick power cables. The cat cowered, knowing from

Barse's frenzied activity that danger lay only seconds in the future.

"We're up to full power. I have one hundred percent on my circuits. The vacuum-brained bastard didn't damage any of my controls."

"We're heading in. The cameras aren't much good for ranging, but Chikako has a small approach radar unit working. We can't calculate distance, but we have direction. Ready the radiation cannon."

"Cannon, aye. The switch is activated. We can fire at least ten times before we have to get a new power plant," Barse said, hoping she was close to the correct number. She had run computer simulations on the switch and its expected lifetime under combat conditions. Ten firings might push their luck past a Schwarzchild radius and into a black hole, but it was still better than firing once and then having to rebuild the *Preceptor*.

The trio worked together to do not only their own jobs but that of ship's commander. Barse had known for some time that Norlin was a good captain. He coordinated well, even if he didn't know everything a seasoned captain did. With the position empty and the computers that might have substituted for him gone, the *Preceptor* almost limped into battle.

"Range looks good. We have contact. We're firing now!"

Barse tensed. She thought she heard Sarov's cry of "now!" through the ship and not over her headphones.

The engines strained as they tried to maintain operating levels. She watched the fissionables in the primary activation chamber slowly vanish. Without the transuranics to trigger the fusion reaction inside the mag bottles, they couldn't excite their more powerful shift engines.

Barse did what she could to change from one chamber to the next as the captured radiation cannon continued to fire.

"Is it doing any good?" she asked Sarov.

She got no reply. She hadn't expected one with everyone on the command deck was busy with the battle. Her real answer came in that the ship was still in space.

Barse toiled mightily, guiding her RRUs and jumping in herself when the robot units fell behind. She swapped circuits, changed equipment manually and struggled to maintain a level of power capable of discharging the radiation cannon.

She must have succeeded. Just as she was certain they were not going to survive because of rapidly lowering levels of fissionables, the cannon fell silent.

She heaved a sigh of relief when Chikako reported, "We got it. We fired two dozen times, and we got it. Nailed it dead-center. I swear, Sarov is a genius. With the information he had there wasn't any way he could possibly target that alien son of a bitch. But he did!"

"What damage did we take?" Barse asked. "I don't see any indications we're in worse shape than when we started the battle. My engines are still in peak condition, and that's what matters if we want to get back to the planet." She looked at the pile of debris around her from discarded equipment left by the RRUs. "Well, not in peak condition but still navigable."

"We took one hit with a small missile. It might even have been a natural meteoroid and not launched from the enemy. We'll have to get a repair unit out to see." Chikako sounded pleased with herself. "The worst damage we have is what Liottey caused."

"The…" Barse caught herself. They had engaged an alien ship and beaten it decisively. She couldn't stay mad at the first officer long, especially remembering how he had been deranged by the CoolinGas. "Are we heading back?"

"I've tried to contact the Port Authority for docking authorization, but all our long-range com units are down. I'm trying to kludge together something. We might get back before I complete the work-around."

"I'll get onto it," Barse promised. "How long a trip will it be back to Porlock?"

"Minimum energy orbit," Sarov cut in. "It's the only data I can get out of the computer that I can be sure of. We can use the time to get back into fighting trim."

"Whatever you say…Captain." Barse let the word drawl out for a couple seconds to show him she didn't consider him to be in charge. Their real captain had been left on the planet by the out-of-control Liottey.

"We'll fetch Norlin," Sarov said with ill-grace. "Until then we can all agree on some things."

"Let's talk about them," Barse said. She was willing to negotiate on any point—as long as the others agreed with her when they finished. They had a mission to carry out, and she wanted to be sure they did it.

Chapter Seventeen

The transporter hummed along and gave Pier Norlin the first chance to rest that he'd had in days. He lounged back in a hard seat and let his eyes close. Sleep eluded him, though. He couldn't relax enough to keep his thoughts away from his destroyed ship and dead crew. Gowan Liottey had not been responsible for his actions, but this didn't make Norlin feel any better.

It had been his command, and he'd lost it.

He shifted to find a more comfortable position on the hard seat and wished this was more than a cargo transporter. He wanted to look at vidscreen scenery racing by outside, even if it were only projections of more distant, lovelier terrain. Had he penetrated the metallic bullet's hull, he knew he would find only pitch darkness and featureless tunnel stretching from one side of the world to the other.

He had given this transporter priority over all others—he hoped. The control board had been simple compared to that on the *Preceptor*, but he had never really worked one before. No matter how simple a computer system, it required time and effort to learn all the intricacies, including the failsafes and redundancies. At these speeds, he wouldn't even be a memory if he smashed head-on into another transporter he had failed to reroute.

Norlin wished he were back in space. There, such things never mattered to him. The *Preceptor* always demanded his full attention and kept him from worrying about details beyond his control. More to the point, he knew what to do. He had been trained for it, and knew the ship's reactions as well as he knew his own.

He pulled the com-link from his belt and pried open the case. Hinky had removed the innards, leaving only a few components intact. Norlin sighed and wished he had replaced the unit at the 'Quator Station. He simply hadn't thought of it.

His thoughts began to travel different paths. He wondered why the genhanced man didn't live in more ordinary company instead of skulking about underground. For all that, he couldn't understand what any of them, human or genhanced, gained by hiding in the transporter tunnels and living off debris.

The transporter shivered and began slowing. Norlin glanced at his watch and realized he had been daydreaming far longer than was good. The transporter had traveled almost a thousand kilometers to the station nearest the alien crash site, and he'd wasted time that would have been better spent planning. He heaved himself erect and rummaged through the equipment he had packed. The 'Quator Station hadn't given up any weapons, so he had to rely on his sidearm for any combat situation.

Everything else was his for the asking. As opposed to his forgetfulness in getting another com-link, he hoped he had requested the right items from the station's warehouses. Returning for the proper ones didn't seem likely with the gen-hanced Bo Delamier and his sister jockeying to take over the government, and the ES post in total disarray.

Hefting a pack, he made his way back to the hatch. The transporter came to a smooth stop, and the door cycled open. Hand on his pistol, he peered out cautiously. His caution was unrewarded because the platform was deserted. The entire underground transporter system seemed deserted. Norlin preferred this to having throngs of people around asking questions, getting in the way, impeding his progress toward revenge.

He preferred it…but still felt uneasy.

He secured the transporter on a siding then hiked the stairs to an upper level. He paused when he heard scurrying sounds. Drawing his pistol, he waited. It took only a few seconds before dark shapes emerged from the shadows and moved toward him on velvet-touching-velvet soft feet.

Two men and a woman from the underground emerged under the circle of light from a single halogen lamp splashing down on the platform. They were indistinguishable from those he had encountered earlier.

"There he is!" one cried, pointing in his direction. Norlin's finger tightened on the pistol's firing stud. He held off and pressed his back against a cool wall. Needless killing served no purpose.

"I'm a friend of Hinky's," he shouted. "I know Skeggon and Meli." With his free hand, he fumbled and found the goggles they had given him for seeing in the dark. He held them up. "They gave me these."

The trio paused and discussed the matter. The woman, who had filthy, matted black hair, pointed a gnarled, broken finger in his direction.

"What you do here?"

"I'm going to the surface. I have a…mission," he finished lamely. He knew what Skeggon and the others thought about ESers. Norlin still wore his uniform, and the pistol in his hand was standard issue.

"Why should we believe you? The ESers come down here and shoot us like rats."

"I'll leave you alone. I'm just passing through." Norlin looked around for a safe retreat. He had the feeling there might not be one unless he convinced these three of his honorable intentions. A sense of presence around him made him wary. These three weren't the only ones on the platform.

He just couldn't see the rest.

He dropped the goggles over his eyes and waited for the small battery to power up the ceramic lenses. The light glared and almost blinded him, then adjusted properly. He saw into the shadows behind the three in the middle of the platform and shuddered. No fewer than a dozen men and women lurked there, all with weapons of some sort. His pistol probably provided more firepower than the lot of them, but he couldn't take the chance.

"I have no quarrel with you. I just want to get to the surface."

"You know Hinky?"

"Not well. I don't know Meli or Skeggon too well, either, but I do know Skeggon worries about her going to Isotope City. He thinks she's got another lover there."

The trio put their heads together again. He saw a man in the shadows signaling. His fingers worked in a code Norlin couldn't decipher.

"Hinky says you're all right. He's building something out of circuitry you gave him."

Norlin stepped into plain view—and knew he'd been lured into a trap. A half-dozen tiny lasers cut holes in his pants legs. Two found flesh and left stinging wounds in his calves. He tried to dodge back, but the injuries robbed him of mobility. He crashed flat on his belly as he worked to get his pistol swung into action.

"He's got a burner! Run for it! Get 'im! Kill him!" came the conflicting cries from all around. Norlin cursed his inattention. There were scores of the Undergrounders. They had circled him, effectively cutting him off from retreat to the transporter.

"I don't want to fire," he called. "I'm an officer in the Empire Service, but I have no desire to arrest you. I just want to get to the surface!"

They paid him no attention. The low-power laser beams continued to seek out a vital organ or a vulnerable, debilitating spot on his body. Norlin pressed the firing stud on his pistol. It hummed and sent a beam blasting into the darkness. Using his goggles, he could have wiped out the men and women in a matter of minutes. He chose to chip off bits of concrete and steel columns above their heads, driving them deeper into the tunnel system.

Rolling, he came to hands and knees. A sharp pain burned in his side—a beam had touched his rib. He jerked around and fired instinctively, heard a strangled gasp. Someone had died at the other end of his laser.

The butt of his pistol had begun to warm. He knew he had to let it recharge or he would soon be spitting sparks and completely at their mercy. He relaxed his arm, rolled onto his side and kept rolling until he crashed into a wall. Slithering along like a snake, he made his way toward a spot where he hoped to find stairs to the surface.

The corridor was blocked with plastic crates. He sat up and looked behind him. More people than he could count advanced on him. The idea of wantonly killing those civilians he was entrusted to protect kept him from firing wildly. Besides, even if he could fire rapidly enough, he had no chance of getting all of them before some overwhelmed him.

He sucked in a deep breath, pushed the minute points of pain from his mind and tried to relax. He remembered how he had responded when Trahnee spoke to him. The flood of relaxation let him see the answer to his problem.

Norlin fell flat on his belly again and fired into the crates until his laser turned uncomfortably hot and he had to drop it. In the tight corridor, the plastic-carbon composite crates caught fire and quickly filled the area with noxious black smoke. The long corridor acted like a chimney and pulled the choking vapors directly toward him until his eyes watered and he couldn't breathe. He pressed his face against the flooring and let the hot gases rush over him. The small layer of trapped oxygen near the floor kept him alive.

He wasn't so sure about the others. Some ran off screaming. They didn't get far before they crashed to the floor, wiggling weakly and making unpleasant mewling sounds. Others died on the spot, the air ripped from their lungs. Norlin peered around the corner and saw the molten mass of plastic bubbling on the corridor floor.

Waiting didn't seem like a good idea. Holding his sleeve over his nose, the goggles protecting his eyes, he dashed forward. The sticky melted plastic clung to his boots, holding him back. He kept moving until he got to the end of the corridor. The door had been barred on the inside—the Undergrounders were in complete charge at this station, he realized. Getting the equipment—and the transuranics—from the cargo transporter might be impossible.

Norlin had no choice but to push on and trust that he could fight his way back after he located the alien ship.

He laughed harshly as he pushed into the soft warm sunshine outside the station. If the alien crew still lived, he might never have to worry about refitting their ship. He'd have a fight far worse than the one he'd just gone through simply to get inside.

He used the laser pistol to make sure the Undergrounders couldn't close the door and bar it again. He rayed the heavy metal door until important parts puddled. The stench of toxic vapors from the destroyed plastic composite crates made his eyes water and his nose run, but he no longer felt the /caustic fumes in his throat. He was glad to leave the entrance behind and start across the idyllic countryside.

After five minutes, he barely remembered the tense skirmish underground. Sunlight fell warmly on his face and erased the strain. The grass crushed moistly under his boots and added a spring to his step to such an extent that he knew he could beat a thousand aliens by the time he hiked to the top of a small rise and stared down into the bowl of a verdant, tree-spotted depression.

A burned area in the center showed where the alien scout ship had crashed. Norlin saw large pieces of hull scattered for hundreds of meters. Some had sheared off the tops of trees as they sailed through the air from the impact and others had caused minor brush fires that had burned out of their own accord.

He hunkered down to keep from outlining himself against the clear azure sky. He didn't know if anyone had survived the crash, but it looked unlikely from the extensive damage he saw.

What the fragile-appearing, spidery aliens could endure was still unknown. On Sutton II they had fought long and well under adverse conditions. However, they'd had full use of their robot fighting machines. The few pitiful other specimens he had come across had all perished inside their tanks. For all he knew, they might be ferocious hand-to-mandible fighters.

Norlin tried to suppress a river of gooseflesh rising along his spine. He knew nothing about the aliens, except for their implacable killing. What part of the spectrum did they use to see? Smell? Was it acute or ineffectual? Hearing? They might be listening to his heart rapidly beating as he pressed into the ground. Or did they have senses he couldn't even imagine?

Humans could be genetically altered for special talents—how Trahnee affected him was an unknown. But what might an alien evolving under another sun be capable of?

Norlin wiggled forward until he came to a thick copse. Hidden from sight, he dared stand and make his way through the trees. Hiding behind a thick bole, he peered around at a piece of the alien spacecraft in the center of a small meadow where tiny fires from the crash still burned.

Nothing stirred. He jumped when a bird cheeped and tried to escape a marauding snake in the tree above him. Norlin sank to one knee, head bowed and heart at the point of exploding. He was too keyed-up. Forcing himself to calm, he skirted the clearing. The alien pilot had not attempted to retrieve this major portion of his downed ship; Norlin found no trace that the huge plate had been touched since coming to rest.

He explored closer to the twisted spaceship hull. A mounting sense of foreboding kept him from rushing out to examine it. Again a sense of presence told him he was not alone.

He drew his laser, checked the charge and knew he had to be doubly careful. If he had a dozen full-power shots remaining in the weapon, he'd be lucky.

He didn't feel lucky. He felt scared.

Circling gave him a better picture of the alien vessel—and it told him his dream of refitting the craft and rocketing into the center of the Death Fleet with a load of fissionable material was out of the question. This scout ship would never lift again. The engine compartment had struck first and been ripped apart so that it lay twenty meters away from the rest of the ship. After seeing the mangled tail section, he periodically checked his wrist sensors for radiation leakage. The rest was holed and looked like metallic lace. This was not a spaceworthy ship and never would be again. Norlin wasn't even sure he could get it to blow up on the ground. It had sustained so much damage that what remained must be inert.

Advancing slowly, making full use of the ground cover, he gained the edge of the ship's forward compartment. He peered inside. Darkness. Nothing moving. He held his breath as he slipped into the ship to explore and hunt down the pilot.

The passageway had buckled and bent, forcing him to duckwalk to the cockpit. The equipment had been smashed beyond recognition—if he could even identify the function of the electronics. None of the controls carried markings of any kind. He put on the goggles Hinky had given him and tried those. No lettering appeared. Either the aliens used a system depending on some sense other than sight for information or they had no need of marking important equipment.

Norlin pushed aside part of the crushed control panel and examined the maze of wiring underneath. The aliens used foptic cable in ways similar to that aboard the *Preceptor*. The thin optical fibers carried light-frequency information throughout the ship. He wanted to explore further and study the radiation cannon firing system. Any data on it would prove useful.

As he thought of it, he fought down a pang of regret. His ship had been destroyed in combat by an alien ship using the radiation cannon. They had never used the device without crippling themselves every time they fired it.

What would Barse have done with this ship? Chikako? Sarov? They would rip it apart until every fastener gave up its secret.

He wished he had a recording device of some sort. Photos for computer analysis would be useful later. He was moving around to get a better view of the control boards when he heard a scraping sound outside the hull.

Norlin scooted to a hole blown in the side and looked out. A spidery creature, dragging two of its eight appendages behind it, crossed the open area he had avoided. The creature hugged a small tree limb to its hard body.

Fear froze him. Where did those large black compound eyes look and what did it see? He couldn't tell. The alien had been out hunting and only now returned. Norlin slid the laser from its holster. Cold rage mounted inside him. This being and others of its species had murdered millions, perhaps billions, of humans.

Even more immediate, they had destroyed his ship and *his* crew.

Just as the alien levered itself up into the ship using the tree limb as a crutch, Norlin attacked. He shifted his aim at the last possible instant, burning away the wood instead of the alien's legs. The alien let out a shrill chittering sound as it tumbled onto its side.

Before it could scuttle off, Norlin slid through the hole in the hull and fell heavily to the ground. He leveled the laser pistol at the alien in an obviously threatening gesture.

Four legs—two of them not legs but arms with tiny hands, he now saw—moved outward in what he assumed was a gesture of surrender. It looked as if the alien prepared for crucifixion.

"Move away from the ship. Get into the sunlight where I can see you," ordered Norlin. The alien didn't move until he motioned with the pistol.

Only when he saw the spindly legs and the feeble arms did he relax. The spider being was unarmed and virtually naked except for a simple medallion driven with cruel force into its chitinous thorax. Norlin thought the small round gold medal might be rank insignia or other identity identifier but wasn't going to approach close enough to check.

Holding the pistol on the alien gave him the edge. Moving closer took away that advantage.

Only then did he realize he had captured one of the enemy. Living, breathing, talking, the alien meant more to the effort against the Death Fleet than anything else he had done.

The radiation cannon's capture had been significant, but it meant nothing in comparison to this seizure. Humanity now had weapons that worked against the aliens and must eventually be installed in ES cruisers. The cannon only added to an already significant capability.

With the captured alien, the Empire Service could find out directly about their enemy, how they thought, what drove them to genocide—everything.

Including the location of their home world. More than anything else, Pier Norlin wanted to carry the war to the aliens' home world. He wouldn't enjoy turning it into a blackened cinder, but it would help mute the image of Neela Cosarrian dead in his arms. It might even help him forget the devastated worlds plundered and left behind.

Nothing could repay them for the destruction of his ship and crew, however.

"You are going to tell me everything," Norlin said to his silent prisoner, motioning with the laser pistol. "Perhaps not now, but soon. I assure you of that!"

Chapter Eighteen

Pier Norlin slowed as he neared the entrance to the underground transporter system. The door still hung open, mostly turned to slag by his pistol, but strange noises from inside made him cautious. He gestured to the alien to halt. The spider being hunkered down, pulling its two injured legs up under its thorax. Norlin refused to let the creature use another crutch; it couldn't escape or rush him with such limited mobility.

He slipped up beside the doorway and pressed his back against the wall. Laser pistol clutched tightly, he spun, leveling it. No target presented itself. He flipped down the goggles and peered into the dimly lit interior. Nothing moved, but the sounds that had alerted him persisted.

The spider alien trembled when he faced it again. He wondered what thoughts raced behind those inscrutable compound eyes. As far as he could tell, the alien showed no emotion on its face, but the shaking might mean something other than fear. If it communicated through body language, however, Norlin was illiterate.

"We're going in," he said, hoping the alien could understand. For all he knew, it might be able to understand perfectly—or even talk to him, if it chose. After all, the aliens knew enough about humans to sabotage deep-space sensors and must intercept communications to know about defensive capabilities.

He didn't bother adding that he was using the creature as a decoy, because the alien was undoubtedly smart enough to understand that. If the Undergrounders attacked, he wanted the alien to be in front of their lasers. He didn't want to expend such an important prisoner foolishly, but if it guaranteed his own life, he was willing to do it. How many humans had this one alien slaughtered? Norlin knew the numbers might be imponderably high.

The alien scuttled off, two injured legs dragging. Norlin tried to detect any pain on the alien's part and failed at this, too. The alien formed a perfect vacuum around itself, communicating nothing. He couldn't even tell if the creature was angry at being captured.

Remembering the suicidal tendencies they had shown in preventing capture of their starships, he had to be on constant guard. If the alien could take out an entire planet, it might be content to sacrifice itself to kill only one other human—Norlin.

They made their way through the now-cooled plastic-melt field on the floor. Norlin reached out to grab the alien to slow it when he heard rustling ahead. The alien turned an improbably hinged arm around and caught his wrist then lifted him with contemptuous ease and threw him through the air to crash hard against a wall. Only by dint of effort did he hang on to his laser.

He rolled onto his belly and brought the pistol on target. The auto-aiming device blinked once as it sent out a red sighting dot. The alien froze. The purpose of the red dot was obvious.

"Don't try that again, or I'll burn another leg off," Norlin said. In a way, he was happy the creature had tried to escape. It was a human gesture and established a basis for later communication. The spider being was not meekly accepting its captivity.

Norlin pointed with his left hand and got the creature heading back down the corridor. When they emerged onto the upper platform, he anticipated an ambush. When it didn't come, he got even edgier. He wasn't a ground combat soldier used to such fighting. He belonged in space, in the command chair running a cruiser.

A knot formed in his throat when he thought again of his lost crew and ship. They had died in space where they belonged—but they had died. That he hadn't been with them rode along with Norlin as a load of increasingly heavy guilt. The alien's scout ship had been devastated beyond repair. How was he ever going to take the fight to the Death Fleet?

The sounds finally made sense to him. He almost cried out in horror when he realized the Undergrounders were trying to pry open the doors to the cargo transporter he had left on the lower level. The transuranics inside could contaminate not only this complex but a quarter of the continent if they were opened carelessly. From the few Undergrounders he had encountered, Norlin didn't think caution was a common trait. They had arrived at the bottom of their society—literally—and had nothing to lose.

Death might even seem a reward to them. They lived off debris on a world dedicated to sybaritic delight.

Norlin herded the alien ahead of him and down the stairs. He checked quickly with the goggles to be sure they weren't going into a trap; the upper platform was deserted. The lower level writhed with furious activity, however. Dozens of Undergrounders used pry bars and their low-intensity lasers to chew at the transporter's tough metal hull in an attempt to steal the cargo.

"Stop!" He fired his laser at the transporter, warming a bit of metal just above where two men struggled with pry bars to lever open the sealed doors.

Many scuttled away. Others swung on him, the dead looks on their faces a harbinger of what might come. They cared nothing about life any longer.

"You're dead if you come any closer," Norlin warned. He tried to keep the alien at the edge of his vision and still watch the Undergrounders. He was confronted on too many sides for comfort.

"There is no need," came a soft voice. "Let him be. He is a good man. He wants only to help."

"Trahnee!" he called. "What are you doing here?"

"I followed you. I had to. Bo is in desperate trouble and needs your assistance."

"I gave him all I'm going to. I should have killed him and didn't—and I could have turned him over to the ES for mutiny. They must know he had something to do with the rebellion."

"That's the trouble he is in. Several rebel leaders have indicted him. Even I cannot get him free. You, though, can speak for him."

"Why me?" Norlin asked, still concerned by the ring of Undergrounders. Their weapons were primitive, but a man could die from a rock to the head as quickly as from a sophisticated cyclic combat laser beam.

"The Empire Service is fond of analyzing battles won and lost. Your part in commanding the robot tank corps has not been ignored. In fact, they see you as a hero of the Empire. Several lower officers have nominated you for the Starburst Medal. Isn't it strange how their enthusiasms change so quickly?"

Norlin smiled wanly. The Empire's highest award for heroism shouldn't be considered for someone who had lost his command the way he had. The *Preceptor* had left without him and been destroyed. All that he had done on Porlock was a fluke. He knew nothing of tank warfare or putting down civil insurrections.

"There aren't many line officers left," he said, remembering how he had maneuvered most of them into fatal situations. That, too, would go against him if any of Emperor Arian's genhanced tacticians studied the records too closely.

"There are none." Trahnee smiled wanly. "That is another point in your favor with the officers who survived. They are not fools. Their advancement would have been slowed by years without your tactical...expertise."

"That's one word for it." Norlin kept his pistol swinging in an arc so he could fire quickly in any direction. "Are you controlling them?"

"They are my allies. I had thought to enlist them, but they cannot be used. Living like animals in the tunnels. Any control I might have over them is tenuous, at best."

"Why don't you just talk to the Empire Service officers?" he asked. Her persuasive abilities would go far in freeing Delamier from his jail cell.

"They are under combat conditions. Few will listen. All wear full battle gear."

Norlin nodded. The troopers had donned their full combat com-link equipment. Trahnee couldn't use her vocal talents, since everything they received was filtered to a monotone to prevent the use of sonic weapons against them. And she was a living, breathing sonic weapon.

"Are they still fighting the rebels? Have they sighted the Death Fleet?" he asked.

"Is this an alien? Yes, it must be. What curious structure. Insect and arachnid. Empire Service scientists will work long hours figuring out its physiology and biochemistry. Since it is still alive, they can also probe its species' psychology and learn something of its motivation before it dies."

Norlin saw how the spider being recoiled at the hint of vivisection. It *did* understand when they spoke, which meant it communicated by sound. All they needed was to get it talking. Given the equipment, a computer expert could put together a translation program in a few hours.

He pushed the spider creature back against a wall and positioned himself so he wouldn't be in difficulty again.

"Get them out of here. Tell them to go rob a trash compactor somewhere else. There's deadly material inside there, and we might all glow for a few hundred years if they break into it."

Trahnee spoke earnestly with the Undergrounders. They grumbled and argued, but Norlin saw that most of them began drifting away as she worked her peculiar genetically enhanced skills on them. In a few minutes, she stood alone in the center of the platform. He studied her closely. The forlorn expression on her face told him she wasn't lying about the dilemma Bo Delamier found himself in.

Civil insurrection, mutiny, rebellion—each carried the death penalty under Empire law. Delamier had bet everything on the Porlock rebels and had lost. Norlin wasn't inclined to help him—except for Trahnee.

He wondered if her persuasive powers forced him into this or if he did it because he sincerely wanted to. He still fought with the feelings he had for her and the knowledge that she generated them in him with her mellifluous words.

"I'll key open the transporter. It doesn't look too damaged. They didn't have long to work on it. We can return to Service HQ and talk to them about Bo. I want to turn this one over to them, too. A little interrogation will be needed, but we can find out a good deal of information." Norlin still studied her reaction, and realized she thought of the alien as a bargaining chip to get her brother free of prison.

"Their Death Fleet has been sighted," Trahnee said. "The entire world is preparing to fight them off, as well as it can after fighting a civil war. Again, you are seen as a savior. You have become a planetary icon, Pier."

"Let's get back," he said, uncomfortable at her praise. He didn't feel the least bit heroic. Quite the contrary. More to the point, he wasn't likely to live to accept any medals from the Emperor because the Death Fleet would destroy the entire world.

Guiding the spider being into the transporter proved harder than he thought. The alien realized that distance from its wrecked ship decreased its chances for rescue when the Death Fleet arrived. If it were caught in the human headquarters when the fleet arrived, it would be annihilated along with them.

He secured the spider being by tying down four legs. He didn't bother with the arms. Long before the alien could work its legs free, he would notice and stop it.

Norlin settled into a hard seat, Trahnee beside him.

"Such an unusual beast," she said. "It understands every word we say. I can tell."

"Is that part of your talent?" he asked.

She shrugged. "How can I say? It is so difficult to know what other genhanced—and ordinary humans—can and cannot do. I do not mean to influence with my words, but I do."

He heard the lie, even though she spoke with utter conviction. He wondered if his personal talent lay in being immune to her lies, if not her persuasive power. Still, he had fallen under her sway before he realized her talent. He studied her in the dim light and saw a lovely woman staring straight ahead, her grey eyes blinking slowly. A vein pulsed in her throat and a tiny muscle twitched in her soft cheek. Otherwise, she showed no emotion.

He reached out and touched her lightly. "You don't have to use your powers on me."

"I find that so hard to believe, Pier." She settled down and didn't look at him again.

He turned sideways in the seat and checked the alien. The spider being sat, seemingly docile and uncommunicative once more. The large black faceted eyes refused to reveal the turmoil that must be raging in the creature's soul, but Norlin knew uneasiness lurked there.

The transporter hummed along on its superconducting rails and, hours later, began to slow. When the cargo transporter finally stopped, Norlin jumped up and ran to the door as it cycled open. On the platform stood an honor guard of Empire Service troopers.

"Sub-Commander Norlin?" asked a third lieutenant who appeared far too young to hold a commission. Norlin shook himself. He hadn't realized how he had aged in experience since assuming command of the *Preceptor*. The lieutenant was, in fact, no younger than he had been when he took command of the picket ship doing research work, yet to Norlin he looked like a schoolboy.

That first command faded into Norlin's dimmest recesses of memory.

"I have a prisoner," he said without directly acknowledging the greeting. "It's an alien who crashed and might give us valuable information necessary to defend the planet. What's the status of the Death Fleet? Status on preparation to defend the planet? What is your Port Authority doing?" He wanted to know it all and only succeeded in confusing the young lieutenant. Norlin took a deep breath and brought his raging emotions under control. So much had to be done and there was so little time.

"Sir, that's all being coordinated from HQ."

Norlin sighed. What would a third lieutenant know, anyway? He had been sent as an escort and nothing more. He had to find a briefing officer, a tac officer, even a weapons officer to get the full information. Even then, they might not know. The alien fleet had undoubtedly scrambled the planetary sensors and complicated any defense Porlock might mount.

"Sorry. I just wish we had more assets in space. Are there any vessels able to achieve orbit?"

"None, sir, except for your ship."

Norlin went cold inside. "It's not likely to do us much good. I watched it destroyed by an alien vessel."

"When?" The lieutenant's eyebrows arched up and wiggled as if they had taken on an independent life of their own. "The last I'd heard, the *Preceptor* just docked at the PA."

"Just docked?"

"Yes, sir. They destroyed an alien ship in a brief skirmish hours and hours ago. They lost contact because of damage to their external com array."

"But the ship used its..." He fell silent. Barse had gotten the switch working! The *Preceptor* now fired as rapidly with the radiation cannon as any alien ship!

"This way, sir." The lieutenant stared at Trahnee but said nothing. They were whisked up to an armored surface transport and taken directly to the Empire Service HQ. It only took a glance around to see it had been badly damaged. Inside, only a few rooms were intact. One had been commandeered as a com center. Mounting a defense with such damaged equipment and poor command structure would be impossible.

He had to try.

"Sir!" cried a first lieutenant by the door. "Captain Norlin is on the bridge!"

Norlin blinked in surprise as the room snapped to attention for him. He hadn't gotten used to being ranking officer. No one in the room sported insignia higher than lieutenant.

He also saw everyone was wearing combat headgear. The com-link for each officer ran through the com officer's board at the far end of the room. He kept Trahnee back because he didn't want her interfering—as he knew she would, given the chance.

"What about the alien fleet?" he asked.

"Sir, we're picking up two small formations, each comprised of ten vessels."

"That's not the main body. Those are only scout ships," he said and frowned. That they had picked up any of the alien fleet was curious. This went counter to the usual infiltration-and-attack plan. He looked over his shoulder at his prisoner. The spider being stood impassively, head stationary. What information did those compound eyes take in? He wished he knew.

He considered having the prisoner locked up somewhere else in case the alien was in telepathic contact. However, if that were possible the alien would've already contacted the fleet and all was lost anyway.

"Can you link me to the *Preceptor*?"

"Of course, sir. This way."

Norlin put on the combat com gear and adjusted it. He was surprised to find only three frequencies available to him. He didn't even have a command helmet with a working heads-up display.

"Sorry," the lieutenant said. "There aren't any full comlink units left. They were all destroyed—along with the officers wearing them."

Norlin nodded curtly. "*Preceptor*, come in. This is Norlin. Report."

The burst of activity took him by surprise. Barse, Sarov and Miza all tried speaking simultaneously. He finally quieted them.

"Engineer Barse, report. I'll get to the others in turn."

"Cap'n, good to hear your monotonous voice again. We'll have the shuttle down for you in a few minutes and rescue you from the gravity well. Liottey's all right. The auto-medic says the last traces of the CoolinGas psychosis are about passed. He'll have some permanent brain damage, however."

"Don't let him near the boards."

"On that score we've had…trouble," Barse admitted. "We're working to repair it. All available RRUs are on duty."

"Never mind that. What of the Death Fleet?"

"Only a small element detected so far, Cap'n. I'd say they're bypassing Porlock in favor of some juicier target."

"Strange. Can you set up a brig? I have a prisoner I want to bring up—an alien."

"Alive?"

"So far." Norlin looked around and saw Trahnee arguing with a young officer near the door. "Get down to pick us up as fast as you can. Land in the square outside Empire Service HQ. Don't worry about damage. There's already enough rubble there to strain their repair budget for the next century."

"Coming down personally, Cap'n."

"Soonest, Engineer," he said absently. He keyed off and went to Trahnee's side.

"Sir, I must place this woman under arrest, also. Her brother is—"

"Bo Delamier," Norlin said. "I know. She's aiding me with the prisoner."

"Sir, he attempted to escape."

Norlin's hand flashed to his pistol as he spun to face the alien. The spider being stood quietly, not a muscle moving.

"Not him," the young officer said hastily. "The rebel leader Delamier. He killed four soldiers. He has been put under immediate execution order."

"No!" Trahnee's voice pitched high. Even with his com gear on, Norlin felt the full pressure of the woman's talent. The lieutenant was unaffected in his gear.

"He implicated you," the officer told her. "He said you were a major part of the uprising and had known of several atrocities committed during the uprising. Delamier said you ordered them."

"Former Commander Delamier has an active imagination," Norlin said. "Trahnee has been aiding me. She did much to prevent unnecessary deaths of Empire Service personnel during the rebellion."

"He also said *you* helped him, sir," the lieutenant said. From the glow in the young man's eyes, Norlin saw hero worship. Delamier had misjudged the officer's gullibility or hadn't known how Norlin had used the 'Quator Station com-link to command the robot tank units.

"Shuttle landing!" came the cry from across the room. "Emergency pickup for Captain Norlin and prisoner."

"I've got to lift back to my ship," Norlin said quickly. "We have to conduct a full interrogation of the prisoner, and I need to be in space to coordinate defenses."

"Sir!"

He looked at the stricken Trahnee. Tears formed at the corners of her eyes.

"Can you get Delamier on a vidscreen for me?"

"There, sir." The officer toggled on a small screen in the corner of the room.

"Hello, Bo," said Norlin. He moved in front of the vid pickup to keep Delamier from seeing Trahnee. "What's this I hear about you killing four soldiers trying to escape?"

"They were only humans," said the genhanced officer. "What do they matter? They got in my way."

"You've been mighty free with your accusations."

Delamier turned sly. "I'm innocent of the charges."

"No one's monitoring this screen," Norlin said. "This is just between you and me."

"Trahnee did it all. She is responsible and framed me. You know it. You're the damned hero of this rebellion. Tell them how she forced me to do it all. The fools will listen to you."

Trahnee held back an angry outburst. Norlin raised his voice to cover the sound.

"You didn't have anything to do with it?"

"Nothing. I've been tricked into looking as if I had. She's dangerous, Norlin. You ought to know that."

"Yes, she is." Norlin toggled off the vidscreen.

"He'll do or say anything to get away," she said. "He has no sense of loyalty."

"And you do?" asked Norlin.

"He's my brother. Do something, Pier. Please."

Norlin hesitated when he heard the sudden commotion in the room. Barse brought in the shuttle and set off every alarm on the planet because she landed so close to headquarters. The entire structure shook as the super-heated exhaust raked the far side of the square. He knew the statue that had given him refuge before had vanished in the plasma jet of the shuttle's engines.

"You can't just abandon him, can you?"

"No. He's my brother!"

"Lieutenant!" he called. "Both the woman and the alien are my prisoners. Form a squad. Escort them to the shuttle."

"Pier, no! They'll execute him!"

Norlin watched the spider being and Trahnee taken from the room. He turned to the first lieutenant in charge and said, "When is the execution for Commander Delamier scheduled?"

"In one hour, sir."

"Change it. Execute him immediately." He spun smartly and left to go to the shuttle. It felt good to be returning to his ship and crew.

Chapter Nineteen

Trahnee cried all the way to the *Preceptor*. Norlin sat stolidly beside Barse, refusing to let the woman's tears sway him. Still, they did. He had ordered her brother's death when he might have mitigated the sentence in some way. It had been a difficult decision, but he thought he had done the right thing. Delamier was a time bomb waiting to explode. If he had worked free of the charges on Porlock, another world would have come under his insidious touch, and Bo Delamier would have never stopped until he had a planet of his own to rule. Norlin knew he had saved countless lives by removing the genhanced man from the universe.

Other worries intruded because he wasn't sure how much control Trahnee had exerted over him. Possibly she had, indeed, driven him to do everything Delamier claimed and then ordered him to forget about his role in the uprising. He might never know the full extent of her power, or what she might have caused him to do.

What he did know was that he had come to love Trahnee. Trying to decide if it was generated by the woman's subtle vocal influence or had just happened drove him crazy.

It might've been best if he had ordered her executed along with her brother.

Barring evidence she was solely responsible for his emotions, he preferred to think it had just happened. And if he was any judge, Trahnee also loved him. He had no idea where their mutual affection might lead. That was something that had to develop over time. Now he had a solar system to defend—and a ship to command once more!

"There she is, Cap'n," said Barse. "Home."

"You've done a good job getting the exterior sensors repaired. How many circuits are still out?"

"Less than ten percent. Chikako is working with two crews of RRUs now to repair the foptic cables to your command chair. It'll be good as new when you need it."

Barse had detailed all Gowan Liottey had done. Norlin shuddered at the nearness to disaster his first officer had taken the cruiser. Still, he didn't want to rewire the command chair to allow either the tactical or the com officers to override. He considered putting a cipher or voice lock on the controls. That posed problems should he be disabled, but it would prevent Liottey or anyone else from usurping command again.

He'd have to look into the matter. Later.

"Put the alien into a brig. You can use the one where Liottey kept you."

"Can I put the cat in with it?" Barse asked. "The recirculation fan isn't good enough there to get rid of the methane Neutron generates. Torture like that might loosen our guest's tongue." She cocked her head to one side and added, "He might not have a tongue. Who knows what the gas might loosen?"

"No torture," Norlin ruled. "See to Trahnee finding decent quarters, too."

"Near yours, Cap'n?"

"Yes." He had no desire to discuss his personal relationships with the ship's engineer.

Leaving Barse and Trahnee to tend to the prisoner, he hurried to the control room. He noted with some satisfaction Sarov had closed the battle locks. He had to pass through double sets of airlocks to get into the small control room.

"Captain on the bridge," chimed out Chikako Miza from her com board as she looked up to see who had entered their inner sanctum. Sarov only grunted, but Norlin sensed the tactical officer was happy to have things return to normal.

"Status."

He spent the next hour going over the damage and how the *Preceptor* had fared during the battle with the alien, analyzing every detail of the fight so he would be prepared for the upcoming battle with the alien fleet. At the end of the long debriefing, he looked over Sarov's shoulder and watched a high-speed reenactment of the engagement on the tac officer's vidscreen.

"You went in blind," he marveled. "A great piece of piloting, Mitri. I'll put you in for a chest-full of medals."

"Money's better," the officer growled, but Norlin saw he was pleased with the praise.

"All you'd do is lose it to Barse at cards. You still owe her two months' pay from the last fantan game."

"That's why I'd rather have money," the tac officer said.

Norlin watched the battle unfold, and saw how dangerous a course Sarov had chosen. Still, there had been little choice.

To have retreated would have meant death. The aliens would have swarmed all over the *Preceptor*.

"Cyclic fire rate is high enough on the radiation cannon for serious combat use," he said, nodding in approval. "We can use it in conjunction with the lasartillery and the missiles."

"We're getting low on some missile types," said Sarov. "They don't have any delay missiles or high-det nukes in stock either at the station or down below. For an Empire Service garrison, this one is terribly provisioned."

"They just put down a civil war," Norlin said, defending them and not knowing why. The pleasure world should never have needed to be fully outfitted for combat in any case, "We'll make do with what we have."

"Barse has requested more fissionables for her ticklers. Without the fission engines, we can't power the fusion torch."

"I know," said Norlin. "Without the torch, we don't have shift engines. Or much else."

He sat down gingerly in the command chair, letting the RRUs work around him. He touched the toggle for ship-to-space station com and explained what they needed. A few minutes of threats, wheedling and rank-pulling got him the promise of the material Barse needed to maintain full efficiency on her engines.

"You're learning, Captain," said Chikako. "Six months ago, you'd never have shouted at a space station commander like that."

"They're not Empire Service," he said. "They play at it, but they're just…not." He took pride in believing he and his crew were the real heart of the Service. The *Preceptor* dealt with direct threats to the frontier—and the Empire.

"Strange data coming in, Captain," Chikako said, her sensors flickering on and off like an electric rainbow. "The alien fleet elements are preparing to shift free of the system. They're going somewhere else."

"What of the main body of the Death Fleet?"

"No contact. No ripples from a shift. No crosstalk between their ships on any of the frequencies I've identified. I think they're leaving without a fight."

Norlin wasn't sure this pleased him. He was itching to get even.

"Keep the robots at work. I want full capability back as quickly as possible. Sarov, run a few problems through your tactical computer to find the best use for the radiation cannon, now that we have it working. Miza, bone up on Empire recognition signals. We're going to have to get help—big help."

He left the control room and went aft to where Trahnee sat with the alien prisoner. Barse had welded the creature into a room; Trahnee spoke to the spider being through a screen grate secured with spot welds over a rectangular opening.

"Does it have everything it needs?" asked Norlin, startled at the thoroughness of the confinement. Even if the alien didn't have two damaged legs, it would have a difficult time breaking through the bulkhead.

"Yes," Trahnee said. "I've been speaking to him." Her voice was soft and dreamy. Norlin's guts churned when she used that tone. He recognized it as her most persuasive sonic attack. What was it about her vocal chords that permitted her to reach directly into the brain and affect him so?

"What?" The idea of talking to the alien shook him from his trance.

"I cannot put his name into our speech. The Kindarians use a complex rank-and-position combination with the individual name. Those change, even when the name remains the same."

"How have you learned so much?" asked Norlin, astounded.

"I simply…ask, and he responds," Trahnee said. "My talents affect him, too."

"Kindar," mused Norlin. He felt better knowing the name of their enemy. "Any idea where their home world is?"

"Not yet. I have difficulty with their mathematical notation. They are much more oriented toward probabilities than we are."

"What do you mean?"

"It's hard for me to say because I don't really understand. They project possible outcomes, then choose the one with the greatest probability for success, no matter the cost."

"They chose wrong when they tried raping our planets," Norlin said, bitterness creeping into his voice.

"I inquired. They have watched us for many years. Almost a century." Trahnee paused, then added, "They saw how we treated other aliens."

Norlin shrugged. Humanity's history with the few alien races they encountered had usually ended badly. Neither the aliens nor the empire had bothered to establish reliable communication. The best that happened was an uneasy truce between the species. He wondered if the Kindar had tried to form any sort of an alliance with those alien races. It did not seem so.

"That doesn't mean they shouldn't have tried talking before devastating our frontier worlds."

"That's not the Kindar way," Trahnee said. "I'm not defending them. Please do not shoot the bearer of bad news. I merely repeat what he has said in way of explanation."

"Sorry. Find out where the home world is. And where we're most likely to find the main body of their Death Fleet."

"Which one?" asked Trahnee.

"There's more than one Death Fleet?" Norlin's eyes widened in surprise. He remembered the thousands of black vessels swooping down, radiation cannon firing and turning life to death beneath the lovely rainbows of slaughtering energy.

"Several fleets, each with a different mission," she said. "I cannot understand the numbers, but he seems to indicate at least four fleets of the size you already encountered."

"He's lying. To space that many ships would require the total output of a dozen worlds."

"He's not lying. Not only can't but won't," Trahnee said. "When I speak to one susceptible to my charms, he tells the truth. Also, he likes me. I can tell."

Norlin put his hand on the woman's shoulder, as much to reassure himself as her. She might be as susceptible to the alien as other humans were to her genhanced powers and never realize it.

"Keep putting the questions to it—him. This is all being entered into the computer for analysis, isn't it?"

"Ask Barse. I have no idea what pickups she placed inside before she welded him in." Trahnee's distaste for the permanent incarceration told Norlin much. She had developed a small friendship—or sympathy—with the prisoner that would have to be carefully watched. He wasn't certain the woman might not find an ally in the alien against the man who had ordered her brother's execution.

He hurried to the engineering section where Barse worked diligently installing the fissionable canisters on her precious engines, and swearing constantly at the cat.

"You do good work, Cap'n. Those bastards over at the space station coughed up everything I need. Oh, they griped a lot, but I think they were glad to get rid of the cargo—and us."

"We might not need full power any time soon," he said, looking over the banks of equipment Barse had stored. He replaced the gutted com-link on his belt with a functional one. He felt better now, able to contact the bridge at a second's notice. "The aliens are turning tail and running."

"Didn't know spiders had tails," muttered Barse. "Or are they more like insects? There is a difference, you know, between spiders and insects. It has to do with the number of legs, at least on human worlds."

"Don't be too disappointed in not mixing it up with them again. I want full shakedown trials with the *Preceptor* in perfect condition, especially using the radiation cannon. No more of this sailing off into battle not knowing if your weapons will even work."

"Thank Liottey for that. I just checked on him. The automed says he'll be shipshape in another week. Or as shipshape as he will ever be."

"As good as ever," Norlin said without enthusiasm. At his best, Gowan Liottey wasn't much of an officer. He couldn't even adequately perform his duty as ship's life support officer, much less stand a simple watch without making serious mistakes.

"Where do we go now?" asked Barse. "No aliens in the Porlock system means our job here is finished."

Norlin's thoughts wandered for a moment, then he said, "Trahnee is interrogating the prisoner and learning a great deal. You have a sensor in his cell?"

"Of course. What kind of space-brained idiot you take me for? I'm not Liottey. Every twitch of our guest's hard-shelled body goes into the computer for complete analysis." Barse cocked her head to one side, "Him?"

"Trahnee thinks our prisoner is male and a member of the Kindar race."

"Know your enemy," she quoted. "Makes it easier to blow them out of space."

"We can't go on fighting them by ourselves," Norlin said. "We need to take this directly to the top command. I don't know if Admiral Bendo contacted Empire Service on Earth. We're going there," he said, coming to a decision even as he spoke.

"Not getting the chance to blow a few of the spiders to hell and gone has affected your head," Barse said. "Or is it that fancy genhanced ass of hers?"

Norlin turned cold. "That's none of your business."

"It's all our lives if you make a bad decision because she told you something, if you follow my orbit. Don't think I don't know what she can do with that golden voice of hers. I checked back. Three revolts. Delamier might not have been far from base when he said she was responsible instead of him. She talks and she persuades, Cap'n."

"I know."

"You also know you're not completely impervious to her, no matter what you think. I doubt anyone is." Barse laughed harshly as she grabbed the ship's cat and began stroking his greasy black fur coat. "Hell, she can even sweet-talk that alien, but maybe not Neutron."

The cat turned green eyes on her, then jumped down and walked away, tail high.

"She can be an important ally because we have to take this to Earth. She's been in Emperor Arian's court and knows people there, the power structure, how to get attention. We can go directly to those who might save us all."

"She was exiled from Earth by the emperor. They might shoot her like you had Delamier removed."

"That was necessary." Norlin's words rang hollow. Had he ordered Bo Delamier's execution to remove a rival for Trahnee's affections?

He didn't know. He just didn't know.

"We might use her to persuade the ES commanders. The genhanced don't seem too bright to me at times, no matter how may times they declare themselves to be geniuses. We're all convinced the aliens—the Kindar—are a threat. Maybe she can talk the emperor's courtiers into sharing our concern."

"Earth doesn't care much what happens on the frontier, but they should," Barse said.

"They will," Norlin said, resolve hardening.

His com-link beeped. He touched the acceptor stud, and Trahnee's voice came out, husky with urgency.

"Pier, I've got the information. He told me where their home worlds are. They come from the Black Nebula. I've given the coordinates to Chikako. We know where they come from!"

He clicked off the com-link and stared at his engineer. "Now we can take the war to them."

"If Emperor Arian agrees," Barse said.

"He will. Trahnee can make him listen. *We* can make him listen."

Tia Barse looked skeptical, but Norlin knew they could do it. The Kindar's savage plundering could be stopped if Earth's might swung against the Black Nebula.

He hurried off to find out the complete details from Trahnee. There was so much to do and so little time. Pier Norlin wanted to get started right away.

END

ABOUT THE AUTHOR

ROBERT E. VARDEMAN is the author of nearly two hundred novels spanning many genres, but his favorites have always been science fiction and fantasy. He has served as vice-president of the Science Fiction Writers of America (SFWA) and also edited the organization's *Forum*. He is a member of the Western Writers of America (WWA) and the International Association of Media Tie-in Writers (IAMTW), serving as a judge for that organization's 2007 Scribe Award, and is also a member since its inception in 1979 of the informal group First Fridays, founded by mystery writer Tony Hillerman. For the past five years, he has worked on the editorial staff of four fantasy football magazines and is co-editor with Joan Saberhagen on the Baen Books anthology *Mask of the Sun: Golden Reflections*. As a member of the Coalition for Excellence in Science Education, Vardeman served as consultant to the New Mexico State textbook advisory board in 2003.

ABOUT THE ARTISTS

BRAD W. FOSTER is an illustrator, cartoonist, writer, publisher, and whatever other labels he can use to get him through the door! He's won the Fan Artist Hugo a few times, picked up a Chesley award and turned a bit of self-publishing started more than twenty-five years ago into the Jabberwocky Graphix publishing empire. (Total number of employees: 2.)

His strange drawings and cartoons have appeared in over two thousand publications, half of those science fiction fanzines, where he draws just for the fun of it. On a more professional level, he has worked as an illustrator for various genre magazines and publishers, the better known among those being *Amazing Stories* and *Dragon*. In comics he had his own series some years back, The Mechthings, and he even got to play with the "big boys" of comics for a few years as the official "Big Background Artist" of Image Comic's *Shadowhawk*.

Known throughout the world (though most of the world doesn't know it yet) for his intricate pen-and-ink work, it is possible you've seen more of work in titles as varied as *Cat Fancy*, *Cavalier*, or *Highlights for Children*. Most recently he has completed covers for a couple of Yard Dog Press books, illustrations for magazines such as *Space & Time* and *Talebones*, illustrations for the first of Carole Nelson Douglas' Cozy Noir Press books on Midnight Louie, and has even managed to work a dragon into the official poster for the 2003 Tulsa Oktoberfest!

He spends huge sections of the year with his lovely wife Cindy showing and selling his artwork at festivals and conventions around the country. Check out his website at www.jabberwockygraphix.com for the latest news!

CHRIS CARTWRIGHT is a computer artist who uses 3D programs and paint programs to create her works. Although she creates covers for any type of story, her favorites are fantasy, sci-fi and horror. She originally became interested in web design, which she went to school for, but after taking some art classes, found a new passion. Besides Zumaya, Chris has also created covers for *Apex Digest*, Outskirts Press, *Penwomanship*, *Whispers of Wickedness*, *Midnight Street*, *Insidious Reflections* and many other publishers and authors.

If you are a writer or publisher and are in need of a cover artist or illustrator, you may contact Chris at digitellart@yahoo.com or visit her website at http://www.digitelldesign.com.

Printed in the USA
CPSIA information can be obtained
at www.ICGtesting.com
LVHW091038131123
763772LV00019B/131